Live the Dream...

This is the last and final volume of the Bread Sister Trilogy, three historical fiction novels which tell the story of Maggie Callahan's struggle to survive in the American wilderness during the turbulent years of the American Revolution.

In this tale, Maggie battles cruel winter winds and icy temperatures as she and the old mountain man Jake Logan search through the ruins of the abandoned Seneca Indian village where she was held captive, hoping to pick up the trail of the Ragpicker, the old witchy-woman who stole away Maggie's little boy, Hoot Owl.

Maggie's tale is a rich blend of heart-pounding adventure, intriguing mystery and good, old-fashioned storytelling, created especially for children and dreamers of all ages.

Up The Frozen River

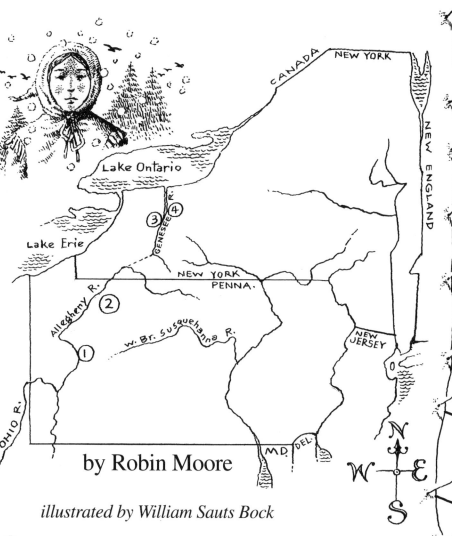

by Robin Moore

illustrated by William Sauts Bock

① FRANNY'S TAVERN IN KITTANNING
② RORY'S CABIN
③ LITTLE BEARD'S VILLAGE
④ CEDAR SWAMP

LIBRARY OF CONGRESS CATALOG NO.

ISBN

Published by
Groundhog Press
Box 181
Springhouse PA 19477

This book is dedicated to my brothers and sisters:

Michael Moore

Dave Moore

Linda Moore Gramley

Diane Moore Price

Who share the hopes and travail of our generation. May the family tree flourish...

Table of Contents

Introduction

Welcome, dreamers of all ages.

In these pages, we will be stepping back in time, into an era when North America was a vast wilderness, populated by wild animals and wild people. A great deal has been written about our frontier grandfathers, the men who subdued the wilderness. But not enough has been written about frontier women, women like Maggie Callahan. Maggie's story is a combination of historical fiction, heart-pounding adventure, and good, old-fashioned storytelling, created especially for those who still live the dream. I hope you enjoy reading it as much as I enjoyed dreaming it up.

This book is the last in The Bread Sister Trilogy, a three-volume series which tells the story of Maggie Callahan's adventures in the wilderness regions of what is now Pennsylvania and Up-State New York, during the turbulent years of the American Revolution, from 1776 to 1780.

Even though Maggie is a fictional character, both adults and children have written me over the years, insisting that she is as real to them as the historical characters they read about in their history books. I think she would be pleased to hear that.

Maggie certainly is alive for me, even if she only exists in the world of the imagination. Whether she is "real" or not, I have learned a great deal from her while we have been making these books together.

One of the most important things she has taught me is that it is not my job as a writer to tell my characters what to do. To be really alive, Maggie must have a life of her own and the freedom to live it as she chooses, without my interference. It's true, as a writer, I can lure her into my story. I can give her a problem to solve, but it is her job to solve it, not mine.

My job is to enter her world, on her terms, and allow her to act as my guide, fully immersing myself in the flow of the story, faithfully writing down what I have witnessed. This is so much more interesting than "making up" stories. Maggie and her compatriots have done a much better job on this series than I ever could have done on my own.

Strange events occur when a writer works in this way. For instance, After I had completed *The Bread Sister of Sinking Creek,* the first book in the series, I was doing some genealogical research into my family's history. I was surprised to find that I had a great great great grandmother who was a

Scotch-Irish frontier woman, similar to my "fictional" character. What's more, I was astonished to learn that her name was Maggie. She married John Calhoun and her married name was Maggie Calhoun. She lived on a 160-acre farm at the foot of Bald Eagle mountain, just a few miles from the location of Maggie's "fictional" cabin in Centre County, Pennsylvania.

A meaningless coincidence? Perhaps.

But there's more. While I was looking over an old map of the region, I discovered that Sinking Creek, which runs right near Maggie's cabin in *The Bread Sister,* was actually called Sinking Meadow Creek. At the place where the McGrew's had their mill, a small notation on one of the old maps I found at the Centre County Historical Society refers to this spot as "Maggie's Dip." There is a steep dip in the road there. I've often asked myself: Who was this Maggie, to have dip in the road named after her? By some strange coincidence, this is also the very spot where my wife picked me up hitchhiking on the day we met. Maybe the real dip in the road was me.

I have often wondered: Are these just random events, meaningless coincidences, things which have no possible relationship to each other?

I don't think so. I think that the lives of our ancestors still echo within us, in some deep, rarely-explored region of the imagination. I believe that if we listen very deeply, we can hear the echoes of the lives that were lived before us. In any case, I like to believe that some remnant of my frontier ancestors' lives still exists in these stories of Maggie Callahan.

As I mentioned before, this book is the third in a series. It's not necessary to have read the previous two books in order to enjoy this one. But it may be helpful for me to give you a brief summary of Maggie's previous adventures, so you can more fully enjoy the tale told in *Up The Frozen River.*

In *The Bread Sister of Sinking Creek,* we met Maggie Callahan, who was then fourteen years old and living in the old family house on Spruce Street in Philadelphia. The year: 1776.

Because her mother had died of the fever and her father was away at sea, Maggie decided to push westward, into the wilderness of Central Pennsylvania, in search of her only remaining relative: Her Irish Aunt Franny. Franny had left Philadelphia years before to stake out a homestead with her husband, Thomas, in the wilds of the Seven Mountains Region.

But when Maggie arrived there, she found that her aunt and uncle had moved on, headed further west, leaving behind an abandoned mountainside cabin. But her aunt had also left her a strange inheritance: A leather pouch containing the Great Callahan Spook Yeast, the secret for baking the Callahan Bread, passed down for seven generations in Maggie's family. Wearing the pouch on a leather cord around her neck, Maggie nurtured the Spook Yeast, giving her a place on the frontier as the Bread Sister. Having no family, she was forced to hire herself out as a servant to the McGrew family who ran the mill along Sinking Creek.

After surviving the dangers of a flashflood, a cabin fire, a snow storm and and the clumsy advances an over-zealous suitor, Maggie broke free to make her way in the wild world with the help of Jake Logan, a reclusive mountain man who had a strong dislike for civilization but a real weakness for fresh-baked bread.

Hardened by two years on the frontier, Maggie pushed further west in "Maggie Among The Seneca," searching for her lost aunt, only to be captured by Seneca Indians and carried up north, to the Seneca town called Little Beard's village, where she was adopted, married and birthed a child among the Seneca, a baby boy named Hoot Owl. Maggie settled into village life with the help of an English-speaking French captive known as Frenchgirl. Frenchgirl's brother, Firefly, was to become Maggie's husband for a short but rewarding time.

But trouble was on the horizon. During an elk hunting trip in November of 1778, Firefly was attacked and killed by wolves. When she and Frenchgirl returned to their village, Maggie's life was struck a further blow when General John Sullivan's Colonial Army came in September of 1779 and burnt the village to the ground, leaving the Seneca to face the winter without provisions or shelter.

It was on that day of smoke and fire and confusion that Maggie lost Hoot Owl. Maggie had wrapped him in a rabbitskin blanket and run down into the thicket by the river to hide. Pursued by a British Army Officer hungry to ransom Maggie off as a captive, she was forced to give her child into the care of an mysterious old Indian woman who the Seneca called the Ragpicker. The old woman was said to be a witch, with magical powers. She lived with her pack of wild dogs down beyond the garbage heaps on the outskirts of the village, living on whatever she could scavenge.

As Maggie was pursued by the British soldier, she ran into the old woman. Without a word, the hag snatched Hoot Owl from Maggie's arms and hurried off into the woods to hide him. That was the last Maggie saw of her baby.

She managed to elude both the British and the Colonial soldiers. After the armies moved along, Maggie searched the smoking ruins of the village, and the woods and fields beyond, but she never found a sign of the old woman or the little boy.

With the cruel November weather at her back, Maggie headed downriver, stole a canoe, and paddled downstream to her Aunt Franny's Tavern on the banks of the Allegheny, in the town of Kittanning, just north of Fort Pitt (The present-day site of Pittsburgh.)

Of course, Maggie never intended to abandon her son to the old woman. She knew that sometime in the future, without knowing just when, she would find her little Hoot Owl. At last, in the winter of 1780, after she had been recovering at the tavern for three months, she couldn't wait any longer. It was time to go back and find what she had left behind.

Which brings us to the story told in this book.

Like the other volumes in this series, *Up The Frozen River* is designed to be read aloud in the old-fashioned tradition of family evenings by the hearthfire.

Enjoy the story. Live the dream.

Chapter One

It was a bitterly cold night in February 1780, deep in the heart of the Western Pennsylvania Wilderness.

Everywhere, the hand of winter was on the land: In the dark hemlock woods, the snow was drifted deep, shaped and scoured by the wind. The creekbeds and swamplands were choked with ice. Even the great Allegheny River was frozen, hard as iron.

But Maggie Callahan and Old Jake Logan were warm enough. Tonight they were camped in a sheltered stand of hemlocks along the banks of the river, fifty miles north of any farm or settlement, out in the great beyond, where only wild things go.

The red-haired girl and the old mountain man had been traveling hard for seven days now, following the winding course of the river as it took them north, back to the Seneca Indian Country, back to the land of dreams and memories and ghosts, back to Little Beard's Village, where Maggie had been held captive the year before.

There, in the fire-blackened remains of the Seneca town, they would look for signs: for owls and wild dogs and pointy-toed moccasin tracks in the snow. They would do what they could to pick up the trail of the Ragpicker, the old Indian woman who lived with her wild dogs in the thicket down beyond the town dump. They would do what they could to recover what Maggie had lost.

Maggie knew that what they were doing was crazy: Setting off in the dead of winter like this, trekking upriver, not sure of where they would end up or what they would do when they got there. If they had any sense, they would be back at Aunt Franny's tavern, basking before the hearthfire, drinking mulled cider and telling stories.

But somehow Maggie knew that it would have been even crazier to remain behind. In the early weeks of winter, Maggie had laid awake many a night in the sleeping loft of the tavern, listening to the wind howling outside and knowing that somewhere out there, in all that cold and whiteness, her little boy might still be alive. Sometimes she pictured her boy, huddled in the arms of the Ragpicker as the old woman poked through the snowy garbage heaps, looking for something to eat.

At last, the agony of waiting became too great. In late January, after the worst of the storms had passed, she talked the old man into going upriver with her. Actually, Jake didn't need much persuading. The old woodsman had been restless all winter, drifting back and forth between Franny's tavern and Fort Pitt, wasting his time in card games and idle drinking and bad company. When Maggie told him what she wished to do, he had the sled packed in an hour.

Of course, Franny and Uncle Thomas were not happy about them going. But they could see that there was no point in holding her. Some of the more outspoken regulars at the tavern predicted that they would freeze solid before they reached the Genesee. But Maggie's mind was made up.

So, in the last days of January, Maggie and Jake loaded their toboggan, strapped on their snowshoes, and headed north, up the frozen river, in search of Hoot Owl.

The weather had been cold and clear, with no storms to delay them. They had made eight or ten miles a day, walking the river trails, sometimes walking directly on the river ice. At night, they camped in ravines and under rocky ledges and in the towering stands of trees that bordered the river.

Tonight's camp was an especially good one: Out of the wind, with plenty of dry firewood and sturdy trees to hang the food bags, safe from wolves. Maggie and Jake had lashed up a temporary shelter there in the trees, thatched with hemlock branches and carpeted with fragrant spruce boughs.

Snug in their make-shift shelter, they sat up by a crackling fire, feasting on a meal of sizzling elk ribs; Callahan biscuits, slathered in bear grease; and cup after cup of tangy sassafras tea, laced with the sweet syrup of the sugar maple.

Maggie gnawed the last scrap of meat from her elk rib and dropped the curved bone into the fire, watching the flames turn greasy and blue.

Maggie was seventeen years old now, and no stranger to danger and hardship. Just as the winter wind shapes and scars and scours the deep-drifted snow, Maggie's years on the frontier had shaped her, making her what she was: Strong-limbed and strong-willed, worth her weight in wildcats. She was built small but strong, with long red hair, eyes that were dark and direct, and the sharply-chiseled features of the Scotch-Irish.

Maggie was dressed for the weather in a combination of buckskin and wool: next to her skin she wore layers and layers of woolen shirts and breeches. Her legs were protected from the deep snows by a sturdy pair of buckskin outer-leggings, fringed with red wool. On her feet she wore a double layer of woolen stockings covered by a pair of thick-soled elkhide moccasins, heavily coated with bear grease. Her buckskin mittens lay near at hand. On her head, Maggie wore a cap made from muskrat fur, crested with wild turkey feathers.

Her outer garment was a knee-length greatcoat her Aunt Franny had made for her from a single red woolen blanket, cut full, with generous sleeves, red fringes at the shoulder seams, and a well-fitted, peaked hood.

On the broad belt at her waist, Maggie carried her possibles: the absolute essentials she would need to survive if she ever got separated from Jake or the toboggan. In an otterskin beltbag she carried her fire-making kit: flint, steel, char-cloth and plenty of dry tinder. On her right hip, she carried her only weapons: A six-inch butcher knife in a rawhide sheath and a short-handled hatchet in a buckskin scabbard.

The old man was dressed similarly, but in a more old-fashioned way. Nearly every article of Jake's outfit was taken directly from the woods. His principle garment was a smoke-cured deerskin hunting shirt which trailed down past his knees. On his legs were buckskin leggings, tucked into knee-high elkhide moccasins, stuffed with deer hair for extra warmth. His bearskin mittens were tucked into his belt.

Jake's outer wrap was a bearskin jerkin with no sleeves, the blue-black hair turned to the inside for warmth. On his head, Jake wore a cap made from the entire pelt of a red fox, the hind legs and bushy tail trailing down the old man's back. The foxy ears were pricked up, open and alert, as if they were still listening in the cold air.

Jake wore his hair unfashionably long, trailing down the back of his bearskin coat. His beard, wild and tangled, was streaked and gray and reached almost to his belt buckle. The mountaineer's face was creased and lined by more than 50 years of wind and weather. But his eyes sparkled, like starlight on gray river ice.

On their toboggan by the fire, Jake had piled his shoulder-slung hunting pouch, with powder horns, skinning knife and tomahawk attached. Leaning against a nearby tree, where his hand could get it quickly, was his long, heavy-barrelled flintlock rifle.

Lashed down on the sled itself were the canvas food bags of dried beans, jerked venison and wheat flour, along with their cooking pots and their bedrolls, woolen blankets and extra changes of clothing and footwear.

With these simple provisions, and a good measure of the hunter's luck, Maggie and Jake could travel through the woods for the rest of the winter, and right up until the green sprigs of spring came sprouting through the snow.

Maggie sat with her back against a tree, staring into the fire.

"What do you think, Jake?" she said at last, "What do you think our chances are of findin' him?"

The old man took his time in answering. He was using his front teeth to pull the last piece of scrappy meat from his elk rib. At last, he dropped his rib into the fire and wiped his greasy hands clean on his beard.

"I spec' he's up there somewheres," the old man said, "if he is, we'll find him. A red-haired baby like that shouldn't be hard to locate. How old do you reckon he is now?"

Maggie counted on her fingers. "He's almost nine months

old. He was just four months old in September, when I lost track of him."

The old man licked his lips. "I don't know if I should be sayin' this —but he won't remember you, you know. If you just left him with the Seneca, he'd prob'ly never know the difference."

Maggie nodded. "Maybe not, but I would. I wanta find him, Jake."

"I kin unnerstan that, I sure kin." Jake let the conversation sit for a moment.

"Now the way I got it figured," he said, " that village is prob'ly emptier than a wolf's belly in January. I hear most of the Seneca have moved up north to Niagara, to winter with the British. I don't see how anybody could stay alive there in this weather. With no food 'er shelter. From what you said, when Gen'ral Sullivan swept through there in the fall, he didn't leave so much as a cornstalk standin'."

Maggie nodded, her eyes turning dreamy in the firelight. "You should have seen how it was before the army came, Jake. You should have seen Little Beard's Village at harvest time, when things were green and growing. It was the most beautiful spot I've ever laid eyes on.

"When I was first captured, when the war party was taking me upriver, I thought they were bringing me out into the wilderness, away from civilization. I thought I'd end up as a slave to a band of savages in a cluster of dirty huts in a clearing in the woods. But it wasn't like that at all."

Jake nodded sympathetically, poking the fire with a stick.

Maggie snapped a twig from a nearby branch and sketched out a map of the village in the snow as she talked. She drew a waving, graceful line.

"This is the Genesee river," she said," and here, this is where they beach the canoes. From this point there is a main road

which runs straight as an arrow to the west, like this, it runs through the whole village, a hundred paces wide. On either side of the road were houses, maybe a hundred of them, and not just shacks, I'm talking about good square-hewn log houses, with cedar shake roofs and real glass in the windows. Each house had a neat yard with herbs gardens and fruit trees.

Maggie drew in broad strokes now. "Out here, beyond the houses, were the fields, hundreds of acres of lush corn and bean

and squash gardens. Pumpkins bigger than a man can lift. Cornstalks twelve feet high with husking ears three feet long.

"And beyond that, out where the horses frolicked and the mules grazed, were acres and acres of lush grasslands. And out beyond that, the forests where we went to collect firewood and hickory nuts and maple sap."

Jake studied the snow map. "Took Sullivan two days to burn it to the ground," he said grimly.

Maggie stared at the map, her vision blurring. A tear coursed down Maggie's cheek and fell into the ashes of the fire. "I was one of them, Jake. I was a Seneca woman, for a while."

Jake nodded. "I think I know what you're sayin', girl. I spent a couple of summers out with the Lenape on the Susquehanna when I was just about your age. I had myself an Indian wife and two little boys."

Maggie was astonished. "Jake, I never knew that."

The old man smiled sadly. "It were a long time ago."

"Do you know what happened to them? I mean, do you know where they are now?"

The old man shook his head. "I think about 'em, now and again, but we just lost track of each other over the years. I spec' the smallpox took them, but I just don't know fer sure."

There was a long sad silence. But just when Maggie was about to press him further, Jake changed the subject.

He gestured toward the map, "So where is this old woman's

hut? What do you call her?"

Maggie nodded. "The Ragpicker, you mean. Well, her place is down here, beyond the cornfields, on the other side of the garbage heaps, in the thicket down by the river. I figure that's where we'll start looking. That's where I saw Hoot owl last."

"Sounds right to me." Jake agreed.

Just then, up in the hills on the other side of the river, they heard the howl of a timber wolf. A moment later, two or three others joined in, raising their voices in a quavering, eerie chorus which made Maggie's scalp feel like it was being pricked by needles.

As if he were reading her thoughts, Jake settled another log on the fire.

"Don't you worry 'bout them," he said, "long as we keep this fire goin' they'll stay clear of us. The last thing a wolf wants is to tangle with a human."

Maggie knew it was true. She had heard many times that a healthy wolf will never attack a human. But still, she was afraid. She remembered the nights when the wolves had come, up along the upper Allegheny, when she and Firefly and Frenchgirl and Cornstalk had been elk hunting last winter.

Then, staring into the flames, she could see other things: images from the past. She saw the butcher elk meat sitting on the rocks and the frozen hide and the wolves' eyes gleaming in the dark. Then she saw the severed stub of Firefly's ankle and the blood that looked black on the snow in the moonlight.

Maggie closed her eyes, shaking off the dark memories. A dozen wolves had joined in now, howling. She could picture them up on the hillside above the river, raising their snouts to the cold stars, howling to the thin crescent of moon that had crested the hill.

"Why do they have to howl like that anyway?" She asked.

"Well," Jake said, "Them wolves howl fer lotsa reasons. To find a mate, to gather their famblies together, sometimes I spec' they do it out of pure loneliness.

"That's the 'empty belly' cry we're hearin' now, calling the pack fer a hunt. They'll set off a a little while and run all night if they have to. If they're lucky, they'll pull down a deer or run down smaller game, rabbits or mice, maybe."

"They live on mice?"

"This time of year, they live on whatever they can git. Listen: if you prick yer ears up you can separate out the male and the females."

"How's that?"

"Well, the she-wolves, they go like this: " Jake tilted his head back and opened his mouth wide, letting out a quavering, high-pitched yowl. "Ouuuuuuuuuuu..."

"Then the he-ones, they go like this:" Jake cupped his hands around his mouth and let out a deep, throaty howl which filled the clearing. "Howuuuuuuuu..."

Up on the ridgeline, the wolves began barking and howling in excitement, as if they were answering the old man's call.

That worried Maggie. "Shush up," she said, " you don't wanta attract 'em."

Then, realizing that she was being foolish, Maggie tried to make a joke of her fears, saying, "They might come down here and ask you to join up with them. You would have made a good wolf, Jake."

The old man grinned, "Naw," he said, "I don't have the teeth for it for one thing."

Maggie smiled. It was good to see Jake like this, out away from the tavern and the soldiers and the whiskey. He was almost his old self again.

"And what about me?" Maggie thought, "Am I my old self again?"

But before she could form an answer, they were startled by a scream that came from somewhere back in the woods, on their side of the river.

"What was that?' Maggie asked.

"I don't rightly know," Jake said. He said it casually, but Maggie noticed that as he spoke, he was reaching for his rifle.

The sound came again, closer this time. It sounded like an animal in pain, a ferocious, pitiful yelping that pierced the cold air.

Jake snatched up his powder horn, snapped open the frizzen

on his rifle and shook a spot of priming powder into the flashpan, snapping it shut.

"Knock that fire down," he said, "I might need my night vision fer this."

Maggie used a stick to collapse the pyramid of logs and stirred the fire down to a bed of glowing coals.

Now the call came louder, fifty paces to their right, heading their way.

"You best climb a tree," Jake said.

Maggie didn't argue. She swung up into the branches of a young hemlock and kept climbing until she was about twenty feet off the ground. Jake crouched with his back against the tree, his rifle ready.

"If you see anything, you let me know," He said.

Maggie prized her eyes back into the dark woods, in the direction she thought the sound was coming from. Her vision was adjusting to the moonlight now. The wind came up, blowing the hemlock branches around, making eerie shadows on the snow. Maggie strained her eyes, peering into the darkness. She thought she saw shapes—the shapes of dozens and dozens of wolves, forming, then dissolving and forming again.

Then, at last she saw something that was not a shadow: it looked to be a lone wolf, hobbling along through the snow, headed straight for their smoldering fire.

Chapter Two

The animal, running with a slight limp, came up to within a dozen feet of the fire and sat on its haunches, pawing at its head, first with one leg, then the other.

Jake stood up and slipped behind the tree, holding his rifle ready. He whispered up to Maggie: "I can't make out nothin' in this light. Kin you see anything from there?"

Maggie climbed down for a closer look, sitting in the branches just above Jake's head. "That's no wolf," she said quietly. "look at his ears, they're flopped down like a hunting hound's."

"Dagnabbit," Jake swore, "my eyes ain't so good in this light. I kin hardly make him out. You figure he's a dog?"

Maggie strained her eyes, watching the poor animal roll around in the snow.

"It's strange," she said at last, "He looks kinda like you, Jake."

The old man's voice took on a sharp edge. "Quit foolin' now. What's he look like?"

"No, Jake, I'm serious. He has a long beard, like yours. He looks to be a bearded dog."

Jake strained his eyes. He had to admit. The dog did appear to have a set of white chin-whiskers. The animal pawed at his muzzle, as if he was trying to scrape away the dangling beard.

The old man watched closely for a while, watching the animal's strange movements. Then, he understood. The old man lowered his rifle.

"That ain't no beard," he said, "them's quills. That dumb dog went and got hisself porcupined!"

"Porcupined?"

The old man nodded. "I've knowed it to happen. That dog bit into the hind end of a porcupine and got hisself a mouthful of quills."

Maggie looked more closely and saw that Jake was right. The poor dog whined and gagged, blinking his eyes and trying to unswallow the sharp quills that had found their way into his mouth and down his throat.

Maggie dropped down beside Jake.

"What do you think will happen to him?' she asked.

The old man shook his head. "He's done for. Them quills is barbed and stuck in there fast, each one of 'em'll just fester and cause his throat to swell up, cutting off his air, so's he can't

breathe. And even if that don't happen, even if the cold weather does keep the swellin' down, he won't be able to eat. He'll starve before them quills will fall out. I spec' in a few days the wolves will find him and make a meal of him."

Jake nestled the stock of his rifle into the crook of his shoulder.

"I best put him out of his misery," he said quietly.

But before he could pull the trigger, Maggie placed a hand on Jake's shoulder.

"Jake, wait. We could help him, couldn't we? I mean, what if we pulled the quills out? He's be all right then wouldn't he?"

Jake lowered his rifle. "Well, maybe so," he said doubtfully, "but first you'd have to ketch him, then you'd have to hold him still while you pull out them quills. He must have a hundred stickers in 'im. It would prob'ly take you half the night."

Maggie stepped forward, "I'm going to try."

The old man shook his head. "Don't be crazy, girl. It just ain't worth it."

Maggie smiled in the dark. "Come on, Jake," she said, "if you had a faceful of quills, I'd stay up all night and help you."

"But I'm not a dog," he protested.

But it was too late. Maggie was already moving forward, talking to the dog in a low, calming voice.

"He'll take yer hand off," Jake warned.

"No, he won't. You said yourself, he can't even bite down."

Jake shook his head and watched as Maggie crept up to the firepit and lifted out one of the charred rib bones. She held it up, as either a weapon or an enticement, whichever was needed. The dog was sitting upright now, his eyes fixed on Maggie's slowly moving form.

"You're not a wolf," Maggie crooned. "You're a dog. We both know that. You know about fires and people."

Then Maggie noticed something hanging from the dog's neck, trailing out on the snow behind him. She could see that it was a hank of busted rope, maybe six feet long.

"So," Maggie said softly, "you ran off from home did you? People there treat you bad? Well, we'll help you, boy."

The dog watched her closely, his body tensed and trembling. Maggie circled around behind him and, ever so slowly, stooped and closed her bare hand around the rope. Then, cautiously, she worked her way along it, until she was less than a foot from the quivering dog. She dropped the bone in the snow before the dog then reached out with a bare hand and laid it on his back, stroking him gently. The hound dipped his head and sniffed the bone.

For the first time, Maggie had a clear look at him. He was a hunting dog, with a tawny, well-muscled body, flopped-down ears and a noble snout. Maggie could see dozens of white quills protruded from the dogs quivering face, tongue and lips. She noticed that a few more quills were driven into his right front paw.

"You poor devil," Maggie breathed.

"Jake," she called, "put that fool rifle down and come over here and help me."

The old man reluctantly set his smokepole aside and stepped up to the firepit.

"If yer aimin' to do this, we best build up the fire," he advised. Without waiting for an answer, he set to work at it: stacking fresh wood on the coals and fanning them into flames.

When the fire was burning briskly, Jake cautiously walked up to the dog and knelt down beside him, running his hand over the hound's back.

"How do we do this?" Maggie asked.

Jake scratched his beard.

"Well, I seed my ol' friend Gimpy Weaver unquill a dog one time. He dipped his fingers in wood ashes to get a grip on them slippery quills and pulled 'em out, one by one."

Maggie nodded. "Sounds good to me. You hold him, I'll yank the quills."

"Are you sure you want to do this?" the old man asked.

"Why, Jake, I never knew you as one to shy away from adventure."

"Don't give me none of that. Adventure is nothing but a romantic name fer trouble. And that's 'zackly what we got here, a four-legged, bristle-bearded combobulation of trouble."

"We'll give it a try," Maggie said confidently.

She scooped up a handful of wood ashes from beside the fire, poured them into a tin cup and set it near at hand. Meanwhile Jake stroked the dogs sleek back and head, shaking his head.

"Yer gettin' yerself an education," he said to the dog, "I doubt you'll ever tangle with a quill-pig again."

The dog followed the man's movements with watery, anxious eyes, but he seemed to understand that they were trying to ease his pain. That was enough to keep him from pulling loose and bounding away. Jake got a firm grip on the rope encircling the dog's neck.

"If I was you," Jake advised, "I'd start on the paw and work my way up to the tender parts."

Maggie nodded. She dipped her fingers in the cup of ashes and closed her thumb and forefinger around a large quill, embedded deep in the dark pad of the hound's paw.

Then, she took a deep breath and gave a quick, sharp tug. The poor dog let out a heart-rending yelp and struggled to pull free. But Jake held him firmly.

Maggie held the quill up in the firelight. It had come free, barbed tip and all.

For the next two hours, Maggie worked steadily, yanking quills from the poor dog's paw, neck, jowls and snout. The quills came out pretty easily. But Maggie had to force herself to ignore the hound's pitiful cries as each barbed dagger was pulled free.

At last, they came to the most difficult task: pulling the quills from the dog's quivering lips, gums and tongue. While Jake held the hound's mouth open, Maggie pulled quill after quill from the tender, pinkened flesh. She noticed that his tongue had swollen to twice it's normal size, almost filling his mouth, threatening to cut off his air supply.

At last, Maggie extracted the last quill from the dog's sore tongue. The dog slumped down into the snow. She gave him a lukewarm pan of sassafras tea, which he drank gratefully, lapping away with his swollen tongue. Then he stretched out by the fire and fell into a deep sleep, snoring loudly.

"Well," Maggie said when she had dropped the last of the quills into the fire, "He's not a wolf."

The old hunter poured himself a steaming cup of tea.

"Prob'ly a farm dog, "Jake said.

"But there aren't any farms around here. What's he doing out up in the hills?"

"He was prob'ly chasin' deer. It happens to farm dogs now and then. They start runnin' deer at nights, while the family is asleep indoors. During the day, they act like a normal dog. But at night, they head up inta the woods and run down them deer. Once they get that chasin' inta their blood, it's hard to break 'em of it.

"Sometimes they run off inta the woods and their masters

never see 'em again. I've even heared of dogs who joined up with wolves and hunt as one of the pack. 'Course, they never forget farms and people and such. That's why he wasn't afraid to come down to our fire, lookin' fer help. A wolf would never do that."

For the first time, Maggie was aware that the wolves were no longer howling up on the ridgeline.

Jake unrolled his blankets and laid them out on the spruce boughs inside the shelter.

"You kin stay up and admire that hound if ya want to," he said, "but I've had enough excitement for one night. I'll see ya in the mornin'."

Maggie stroked the hound's back, "I'll just sit up with him for a while, just to make sure he's breathin' all right."

"Suit yerself," Jake said. And then, in a moment, he was snoring.

Maggie listened to the dog's breathing. It was labored, but regular. She thought he would be all right.

Maggie took off her belt and laid her weapons handy. Then she dusted the snow off her moccasins and rolling up in her blankets, she drifted off, too tired to dream.

When Maggie awoke the next morning, the dog was gone. Jake was already up, setting a kettle on the fire to boil for their early-morning tea.

Maggie twisted in her blankets. "Where is he?"

The old man pointed with his chin off into the woods. "He prob'ly took off huntin'. I saw him get up about the same time I did. He yawned and stretched hisself and then, without so much as a goodbye, he took off for them woods."

Maggie felt a pang of disappointment. She hadn't known what to expect. She hadn't thought that the dog would be hers exactly. But she hadn't expected him to leave so suddenly.

Maggie and Jake had their morning tea and a quick meal of biscuits and jerky. Then they began the familiar motions of breaking camp: they rolled up their bedding, loaded the toboggan and were just about to douse the fire with handfuls of snow when Maggie saw something prancing down through the trees. It was the lost hound, loping along with a dark, limp object dangling from his mouth. As he came closer, Maggie could see that it was a fat porcupine.

The hound trotted up to the firepit and dropped his quarry in the snow. He eyed Maggie and Jake, his eyes gleaming proudly, his mouth bristling with quills.

Jake turned to Maggie. "I've seen smart dogs and I've seen dumb dogs. And that is a dumb dog."

Maggie sighed. "Get me some wood ashes."

Again, she plucked the quills from the poor dog's face as he whined and growled and groaned. She was more expert, and considerably less gentle, than she had been the night before. In an hour she had him de-quilled. She washed his wounds in sassafras tea and watched as the poor dog slumped by the fire, a dazed look in his eyes.

Meanwhile, Jake had not been idle.

"Dog," he said, "Yer gonna get yer revenge."

He drew his knife and proceeded to cook up the porcupine. First he laid the quill-pig in the coals and singed off the quills. Then he skinned the animal, parboiled him in an iron pot and forked him up on a green stick over a bed of red-hot embers.

"I've never eaten porcupine," Maggie admitted as Jake drew the steaming carcass from the fire.

"Tastes a bit like sucklin' pig, "Jake said, "'Specially the tail, almost as good as beaver tail, to my way o' thinkin."

Jake was right. The porcupine meat was sweet and pungent and dripping with savory juices. Maggie and Jake devoured their portions.

As for the dog, he hardly touched his piece. He just mouthed the bones a little bit and looked up at Maggie and Jake with pathetic eyes.

"Think he'll stay with us?" Maggie asked when she had finished her meal.

"I hope not," Jake said, "a dog that dumb could be a lotta trouble to look after."

"No," Maggie said softly, stroking the dog's back. "You wouldn't be a lot of trouble, would you boy? Think of the extra meat he would bring in, Jake."

The old man snorted.

"So what do you say, boy? Are you willin' to leave that wild wolfy life behind and come upriver with us?"

The dog reached out with a swollen tongue and licked Maggie's hand.

"What do you say, Jake? Should we take him with us?"

"I don't know that he's gonna give us a choice, now that he has someone to doctor his wounds. Don't blame me when he starts huntin' black bear, comin' into camp at night with claw marks all over 'im."

"No," Maggie said, "You wouldn't do that would ya, boy? Let's take him Jake. He looks like he needs us."

The old man ran his fingers through his beard. "If ya got yer heart set on it, I guess we can give it a try. The best I can say about it is that it'll prob'ly make a good story someday. But you'll need to give him name. What will you call him?"

Maggie stared into the fire, stroking the dog's back, grappling for a name that would suit him.

"You could call him Porky," Jake suggested.

Maggie made a face.

Jake tried again. "How about Wolf-Bait?"

"Jake, stop."

Then it came to her.

"I'll call him Poordevil," she said, "that was what I called him when I first laid eyes on him."

Maggie patted the hound on the head, "What do you say boy? I'll call you Devilish for short."

Poordevil stuck out his ridiculous tongue and panted, his eyes shining.

"Well, girl," Jake said, "it looks like you got yerself a dog. Not a very smart dog, but a dog all the same."

Maggie stood up. "Come on, boy," she said, kicking some snow onto the fire, "It's time to hit the trail."

Jake lashed down the last of the cooking gear and slipped the sled harness over his shoulders. They strapped on their snowshoes and Maggie led the way back through the trees, toward the riverbank.

Poordevil pulled himself to his feet and, wobbling a bit, followed them up the river trail.

Chapter Three

Over the next ten days, Maggie, Jake and Poordevil fell into a routine of steady travel during the days, camping, feasting and fending off the cold at night. The weather held, cold but clear, and on good days they would make eighteen or twenty miles before darkness forced them to camp.

It was Maggie and Jake's custom to travel single-file, with one person walking ahead, clearing the way, while the other trudged behind, hauling the toboggan by a six-foot rawhide drag-rope which was attached to a leather harness, worn over the shoulders. Breaking the trail was hard work. But so was hauling the loaded toboggan. So they switched off throughout the day, making regular stops to break up the monotony of travel.

This part of the journey became tedious for Maggie and Jake. The countryside was barren, white, lifeless, with nothing to offer the eye but ice and snow and windswept groves of hemlock trees, half-buried in the drifts.

But Poordevil never seemed to lose interest in the landscape. Despite Jake's observation about the lack of game, the hound was always alert, hunting, smelling, running ahead or lagging behind the travelers. He never passed a day without giving chase to some animal, a rabbit or a field mouse. And the fact that he rarely caught what he was after never seemed to discourage him. Day after day, Poordevil pranced ahead, his nose powdered with snow and ice crystals, sniffing his way north.

They were in the upper reaches of the Allegheny now, in rugged, craggy country, where the hillsides rose sharply on either side of the river.

They had taken to traveling directly on the ice. As long as the ice was smooth, the toboggan slid easily and they didn't have to flounder in deep snow on the steep hillsides. They could lash their snowshoes down on the sled and travel, fast and free.

At the beginning of the trip, Jake had been very stern about laying down the rules for traveling on ice. He had taught Maggie to read the ice, just as a literate person can read a book. If the ice was white, Maggie had learned, it was generally safe to walk out onto. But if the ice was gray or black, it was bad ice, too thin or flawed to support the weight of a person.

Maggie knew that walking out onto bad ice was an invitation to disaster. She knew that if she fell through the ice and plunged into the river, she would die in a very short time. Even if Jake managed to fish her out, get her to shore and get her into dry clothing and warmed by a fire, she still might not survive. If she did live, there was a very real possibility that she would lose her toes and fingers to frostbite. Then they would have to use Maggie's hatchet as a surgical tool, sealing off the stubby wounds with a red-hot coal from the fire.

Knowing all this, Maggie had been very cautious about walking out onto the ice. Her first few times, she edged ahead, expecting at any moment that the surface beneath her feet would collapse and dump her into the river. But it never did. In over a hundred miles of walking on the ice, they hadn't had a single mishap.

The ice had always held her weight and the weight of her companions. So, in time, Maggie had come to trust the ice. This was a mistake. Because ice doesn't know about trust and betrayal. Ice is just ice.

An hour before sundown, on their tenth day of walking, the travelers began the familiar routine of searching out a campsite, a place to make their nightly stand against the cold.

Maggie threw back the hood of her blanket-coat and glanced up the meandering river, shielding her eyes from the glare of the sinking sun. Ahead, on the eastern shore, she saw a cluster of spruce trees. She knew there would be shelter from the wind there and dry firewood.

Maggie was walking in the lead, reading the ice, while Jake trudged along twenty paces behind, hauling the toboggan by the drag-rope. Maggie glanced back over her shoulder at Jake. She caught his eye and pointed a mittened hand toward the spruce grove. The old man nodded in agreement, his breath coming in fast clouds.

Maggie was eager to get in off the ice. It had been a long, cold day and she was looking forward to the comforts of camp. Maggie wasn't thinking about the ice beneath her moccasins, or the gray chilling waters that gurgled and swirled just inches

below the soles of her feet.

Instead, she was thinking ahead to the camp in the spruce trees on shore. She could picture herself sitting before a blazing fire, wearing dry socks and moccasins, wolfing down venison stew and drinking sassafras tea.

Then, fifty paces from shore, in a place where the ice looked absolutely trustworthy, it happened. It happened so quickly: There was a sharp cracking sound. Then it seemed that the whole world fell away beneath her as Maggie plunged feet-first into the gray waters of the Allegheny.

The cold water sent a shock-wave through Maggie's body, forcing the air from her lungs. For a long moment, she struggled to take a breath and found that her lungs had collapsed. Then, in a great gasp, she took in the cold air and found herself standing up in two feet of water. Acting on pure instinct, she waded up to the edge of the ice and heaved herself up out of the river.

Maggie managed to thrash up onto firm ice and crawled a dozen feet away from the hole, laying there with her cheek against the glassy surface of the river, panting in great gasps. She pulled herself up on all fours but found she couldn't rise. Her wet mittens and pant legs had bonded to the ice, holding her down. With a terrific effort, Maggie ripped herself free and stood up, swaying on the ice.

Maggie felt her body turning toward shore. She saw the snow and the grove of spruce trees. Abandoning the idea of walking on the ice, her body surged ahead into the shallow frigid water, her feet punching holes in the gray ice as she went.

Within a dozen steps, her outer clothing was frozen hard as iron. Another dozen steps and Maggie couldn't feel her feet. She had to look down to make sure that she was truly walking. All she was aware of in those terrible moments was the wooden feel of her body, the labored sound of her own breathing, and the great gray numbness that was creeping up into her chest, toward her heart and lungs.

Then, at last, she was on the shore, shaking the ice from her feet. She was vaguely aware that Jake and Poordevil were there. The dog was jumping around, barking excitedly, and Jake was talking to her. He was excited too, talking loud and fast, but Maggie's brain wasn't taking any of it in.

Jake led her over to a sheltered clearing among the spruce trees where a large dead spruce tree had fallen on its side in the snow. Jake laid Maggie down on the toboggan and drew his belt knife.

Jake sawed through the frozen wool, wrestling her arms out of the coat and casting it aside where it stood on its own, at a crazy angle, in the snow. The old man pulled a blanket from their bedroll and wrapped her in it. Then, working quickly, Jake cut the thongs that wrapped round and round her moccasins tops, pulling the frozen leather from her bluish feet. Maggie felt powerless to help him. She just lay on her back on the toboggan, trying to talk. She could move her lips, but no sound came out.

It was just as well. Jake was not interested in conversation. He was working rapidly to build them a fire.

First, he tromped down a circle of snow with his mocassins then laid out a platform of branches for to fire to rest upon.

Next, he removed his mittens and worked bare-handed, snapping thin twigs from the downed spruce and carefully heaping them up on the log platform. When he was satisfied, he laid on larger sticks, first the size of his finger, then the size of his wrist, forming a pyramid of dry wood.

Now, Jake reached into his hunting pouch and drew out his fire-making gear: flint and steel. He tucked a dry wad of bark into the center of the twig pyramid. Then he tore a square of charred cotton cloth, placed it on top of a chunk of flint.

Holding it down with his left thumb, the old man struck the stone a glancing blow with his striking steel. He struck once, twice, three times, before a shower of sparks flew off the edge of the stone. One spark fell on the char-cloth and glowed orange.

Carefully, using his body to shield the glowing cloth from any wind, he tucked the char-cloth into a bundle of tinder and carefully, almost reverently, began to nurture the flame, blowing on it lightly to coax the glowing cloth into fire. The bundle began smoking, carrying wisps of cedar bark scent up into Maggie's nostrils.

At last, the bundle burst into flame and Jake tucked it into the pyramid of twigs. The bark and fine branches caught and the fire roared to life!

Maggie's eyes were drawn to flame, as if she could derive some warmth just from looking at it. The flames danced, yellow and enticing. But her body was still cold as stone.

Now, she watched as Jake pulled a lightweight iron chain from their cook sack and used his hatchet to cut stout spruce poles, about as tall as he was. Jake lashed them together with the chain and hung the tripod over the the fire. A moment later, a battered iron kettle swung easily over the flames, filled with snow to melt down for tea water.

Poordevil inched up close to the fire, sitting on his haunches and watching with interest as Jake fed the fire.

Then Jake did a very brave thing. He knelt in the snow beside the toboggan. He lifted the edge of his buckskin hunting shirt and laid Maggie's bare, frozen feet onto the warm skin of his belly. Maggie watched as he squeezed his eyes shut in agony.

"Whoee!" she heard him exclaimed, "Them's is some cold feet!"

It struck Maggie as comical and made her a laugh at little. She was shivering so badly that she couldn't tell the laughter from the shivers. But it felt good anyway.

After Jake warmed her feet on his belly, he took her frozen hands and gave them the same treatment, holding them against his skin, driving the cold from them.

"Kin ya feel anything?" Jake asked.

Maggie nodded. Her jaw-muscles were still stiff with cold, but she felt a little better.

Then, a terrible thing happened. Poordevil had been so intent on watching the actions of the people that he wasn't paying any attention to his own movements.

The hound backed up and one of his hind legs accidentally struck one of the legs of the tripod, knocking the whole works over. The pot of melted snow-water landed squarely on the fire, putting it out.

Maggie could scarcely believe her eyes. A moment before, a warm blaze had crackled and popped there, promising life and warmth. Now there was nothing but a pile of sodden, blackened sticks.

Too stunned to move, Maggie watched as Jake knelt and raked through the wet wood with his bare hands. A few embers still glowed. The old mountaineer desperately blew on them, trying to coax them into flame. But the wood was wet. Despite his best efforts, the glowing sticks winked and went out, even as he blew on them.

The wind came up now, howling through the trees, blowing fresh snow across the fire, and onto Maggie's bare feet. She tried to draw her feet up into the blanket but found that she couldn't move them. All she could do was to lie helpless on the sled while the snow drifted deep around her.

Maggie began to accept that she was probably going to die. Her body was already very cold and it would be a long time before a substantial fire would be ready. If Jake worked very quickly, he might be able to save himself, she thought. But she knew her chances of survival were very small.

Things seldom go wrong singly in the woods. When something goes wrong, it leads to a second misfortune and then another and another.

It was too bad that Maggie had fallen through the ice. It was a shame that Poordevil had put out the fire. And it was a grave misfortune that Jake was beginning to succumb to the cold as well. He had been working with his hands bared to the cold and now his fingers had turned wooden and useless.

Determined to make a new fire, the old man tried snapping sticks from the dead spruce tree. But his hands would not obey him. They would not grip and release. His fingers were frozen too badly. He had to use the heels of his hands to carry individual sticks from the tree to the log platform and that took a long time.

At last, he managed to lay up the fire. Now Jake reached into his pouch and attempted to draw out his flint and striking steel. But the task of tearing off the char-cloth and nestling it into the tinder was much too delicate for his frozen fingers. He tried, but he just couldn't do it.

Poor Jake was shivering so badly that his flint and steel, his tinder and char-cloth, tumbled from his fingers and dropped into the powdery snow. He went down on his hands and knees and searched in the snow, but his eyes were bleary with cold and he couldn't see anything but whiteness and whiteness and whiteness.

Maggie watched all this with the detached eye of someone who is about to die. She should have been afraid, but she wasn't. She wasn't frightened or angry or sad—she was just very tired. What she wanted most was to close her eyes and settle off into sleep.

A part of her mind rebelled against the urge to sleep. Maggie remembered another time when she had felt this way, when she and Deaf Annie were buried in an avalanche back in Penns Valley. She knew then, as she knew now, that this was how a person froze to death, by giving in to the temptation to fall asleep in the great cold. She knew her life depended upon staying awake. But it was no use. Even though she fought against it, Maggie found herself closing her eyes. She slumped back on the toboggan.

In the darkness that surrounded her, she was vaguely aware of sounds: Poordevil was barking and Jake was saying something to her. But then the wind came up, and she couldn't hear them anymore.

Their voices were drowned out by a new voice: the voice of the wind. The sound of the wind in the spruce trees grew louder and louder, until it wasn't just the sound of wind, it was somehow human, singing to her, right next to her ear. Maggie recognized it as an old woman's voice, cracked and brittle, but filled with sweet melody, singing a strange eerie tune. She couldn't make out the words, but she knew from the meter of the song that it was a lullaby.

Maggie couldn't resist the cold any longer. She surrendered herself to the cold wind and settled off into the sleep that comes before the whiteness of death.

Chapter Four

Maggie didn't feel cold anymore. In fact, she felt very warm.

When she opened her eyes, she was surprised to see that she was no longer in the snowy woods by the river. Instead, she found herself in a gray and misty landscape. She had no way of knowing how long she had slept or how she had come to this strange place. But the musical voice surrounded her, like a comforting cloud.

Then Maggie noticed that she was up to her neck in warm, steaming water. Somehow, her clothing had been removed and she was lying in a wooden tub that seemed to be made from a huge hollowed-out log. The water was a dark greenish- gold; the bath was thick with green hemlock branches, brewed into a strong tea. The fragrant steam filled her nostrils.

Someone was washing her feet with a rough rag. As the rag passed over her skin, she felt the warmth returning to her frozen feet. Maggie peered through the dense steam but could only make out the outlines of a person, moving about at the edge of the tub.

She had no way of knowing who it was or why they were helping her. She knew only that she was warm and cared for and that the kind and gentle hands were washing her body, washing the cold from the pores of her skin. At last, she heard the voice singing close to her ear and she felt the rag coursing over her cheeks and forehead and nose and lips and then —

—Then the singing grew fainter and fainter until it was wind again and then the wind was quiet and she heard the crackle of a woodfire and Poordevil's sharp bark in the cold air. But still she felt the gentle movement of the rag across her face.

Maggie opened her eyes. She wasn't in the tub anymore. She was back in the snowy woods, lying on the toboggan. And the rag was not a rag. It was the long pink tongue of the wolfy-dog, Poordevil, licking her face and hands.

Maggie pulled herself up on one elbow and looked around. The sun was down now and she was back in the white, frozen world by the river. Jake had a crackling fire going and a bubbling stewpot suspended over the flames.

"Good to see you up and about," Jake said when he saw her stirring, "I was afeared you were gonna freeze solid on me."

Maggie grinned. She spoke, and this time words came out.

"What happened? I mean, what saved us?"

Jake nodded to the fire.

"It was a trick of the wind. Wind came up and blew through them coals. I found a stick that still had a bit of coal on it. I build up some bark around it, just about burn my fingers raw. But I did it. So now we got ourselves a fire."

"It was the wind..." she mused.

Then she asked, "Jake, you didn't hear anything odd, did you?"

"Like what?"

"Any singing?"

The old man shook his head, "Nope. Jest the wind."

Maggie nodded. "Strange doin's," she said, more to herself than to him.

Then, Maggie told Jake about the strange dream that had overtaken her while she was in the cold sleep. Jake listened quietly and thought it over a few times before remarking, "Sometimes them dreams takes time to figure out and sometimes ya never do find out what they was about."

Then Jake served up a bowl of hot venison soup. Maggie forgot her dream and settled down to filling her stomach.

It was after Maggie had eaten that the thawing pains began. She knew they were coming. She wanted to fortify herself before the fiery torment started on in her hands and feet. Maggie knew that it is not the freezing that pains a person, it's the thawing out.

Jake stayed up with her for most of the night, nursing the

painful stinging of his own fingers, keeping a vigil by the fire and the tea pot. Maggie fought back the pain and wept, despite herself.

At last, after hours of torment, she was empty of pain and empty of tears. She was exhausted. She laid down in her blankets and tried to sleep. But she couldn't. The strange song she had heard in her dream circled through her mind again and again. It seemed to her that the dark figure by the bath had been the old woman from the Seneca village.

She wondered about the Ragpicker, wondered if her so-called magic was responsible for saving her life. She wondered if there was anything the old woman could do, anything anyone could do, to keep a person from dying when their time had come.

"Well," Maggie thought, "Maybe my time hasn't come yet."

Maggie wondered long and hard about the old woman. She remembered the very first night she had seen her. It was on a cold winter's night, about this time of year. This was after Firefly had died and after she had placed his remains in a tree out in the fields beyond the village. Every night, she made a small ritual of trekking out after the evening meal and lighting a fire at the base of the tree, so Firefly would have light on his journey to the spirit world.

She was sitting under the tree one night, staring into the flames of her tiny fire, when she caught a glimpse of some movement in the garbage heaps down at the edge of the field. Maggie knew that there were wild dogs who lived down there, fighting over the scraps of things that people had thrown away, and she thought maybe she had seen a few of the scavengers making their nightly rounds.

But when she looked more closely, she was astonished to see an old person, dressed in dark ragged clothing, poking through the garbage with her walking stick, as if she were looking for something. Maggie watched her for a along time, saw how the dogs milled around and fell back when she gestured with her stick, almost as if they were obeying her.

Later, back at the cabin, she asked her companion, Frenchgirl, about what she had seen.

"Oh," Frenchgirl had said, in that light, lilting accent, "that is the old witchy-one, the one they call the Ragpicker."

Frenchgirl explained that the old woman lived alone in the thicket down by the river, living on whatever she could forage from the refuse heaps. She said that most people were a little afraid of her. Some said she had magical powers. There were rumors that she could kill you with a glance. Or make you sick by blowing a hairball or a sharp bone into your body. Others said that she captured and ate small children for her meals. And still others said that she was simply a crazy old woman who lived off in the woods and wanted nothing to do with the rest of the Seneca.

One night, driven by her curiously, Maggie slipped down through the thicket by the river, searching for the old woman's camp. It was quite dark that night and Maggie had a difficult time making it down through the deep snow.

She heard dogs, fighting over garbage back on the refuse heaps. Moving quietly, she slipped past them and pushing ahead, without knowing why she was taking such a crazy chance. She followed the glimmer of firelight she saw in a clearing in the thicket.

Creeping up through the dried thorns and bristle briars, Maggie could see an open fire burning in the tiny clearing. At the edge of the clearing sat a conical hut, its roof heaped with a mass of hide and bark and garbage. Suddenly, the bark door was pushed aside and the old woman crawled out on all fours and stood up.

Maggie would never forget her first glimpse of the Ragpicker. Her face was lined and wrinkled, like a crabapple left to sour on a tree. Her hair was wild in the wind and streaked with gray. Her shapeless garment hung on her like a ragged tent. And she wore curious shoes, pointy-toed deerskin moccasins.

Then a strange scene took place: The old woman seated herself by the fire, reached into the bosom of her robe and took out a bundle. Maggie watched as the old woman unwrapped it and drew out seven cornhusk dolls, about as large as the woman's forearm, and sat them on the ground around the fire.

Maggie noticed that these were like the child's dolls the girls in the village played with, dressed in bits of hide and cast off cloth, and each one without a face.

As Maggie watched, the old woman stirred a pot of corn soup and spooned out a portion for each doll, feeding them and wiping their mouths with a bit of filthy cloth. Then she took each of the dolls to her breast and nursed it, singing a strange song in an old, cracked voice.

It was then that Maggie remembered where she had first heard the lullaby which had come to her in her dream. It was on that night when she had peered in on the Ragpicker's camp.

Then the old woman had gathered up her dolls and disappeared into the hut, closing the flap behind her.

Maggie had never understood what she had seen that night.

But, one thing was sure. In a week or two Maggie would be back in Little Beard's village. She would go down into the thicket, down to the last place she had seen Hoot Owl, by the Ragpicker's hut. And she would see what she would see.

Was it possible that the old woman and the boy could still be alive? Maggie felt in her bones that they were. But, if so, where would they be and how would they have survived the winter?

There were more questions than answers. Maggie couldn't think anymore. She closed her eyes and slept.

Maggie and Jake didn't make any miles the next day. They stayed in camp and rested Maggie's tired feet and at last on the second day, she felt well enough to go on.

In all of their days of traveling, they hadn't seen another person on the river trails. Now and then, they passed the burnt-out ruins of the Indian villages Col. Brodhead's 600-man army had torched when they marched upriver in September. Just as General Sullivan had done in the country further north, Brodhead destroyed everything in his path: wiped out the cornfields, burnt the bark huts and log cabins, scattering the river people, sending them out into the wilderness to survive the winter without food or shelter.

The river valley was abandoned and sometimes it seemed to Maggie that she and Jake were the only people left on earth, walking alone through the great white world.

Then, an hour before sundown on their twelve day of walking, both Maggie and Jake caught the unmistakable scent of woodsmoked layered in the cold air. Looking ahead, Maggie saw a column of smoke rising from the hillside above the river bend.

Maggie was in the lead, while Jake plodded behind, hauling the sled. Maggie waited until Jake pulled up behind her.

She nodded toward the smoke.

"What do you make of it?" she asked.

The old man's breath was coming in fast clouds. He stopped and looked, squinting his eyes against the glare of the setting sun.

"Could be indins," he said, "Maybe a small huntin' party. In that case, we'd do best to wait until dark and slip around them. I don't think they'd welcome any guests during the starvation time. Besides, they might still be a a little irritated about being burnt out and they might decide to take it out on us.

"On the other hand, they might be white folks. Trappers 'er maybe soldiers. Hard to say. I can't imagine what they'd be doin' out in this weather."

"Yes," Maggie said lightly, "a person would have to be crazy to be out in this weather."

The old man grinned. "I spec' yer right. Why don't you stay here with the sled and the dog and I'll slip up there and see what I kin see."

"Sounds right to me," said Maggie.

They pulled the toboggan up into the trees and Jake slipped on his hunting pouch and checked the priming on his rifle.

"I'll be back afore dark," he said. And then he was gone.

Maggie sat on the toboggan and held the dog, trying to conserve her warmth, hoping she wouldn't have to sit in the cold for too long.

The snow along the hillside was hard crusted and crunched loudly under Jake's snowshoes. He worked his way up as close as he dared. Then he stepped out of his snowshoes, tied them together with a leather thong, and slung them over his left shoulder. It was slow travel from there on out but Jake took his time, working his way up the side of the hill, meaning to come up on the camp from behind.

After a long climb, Jake peered down. Fifty feet below, dug into the side of the hill, was a neat log cabin, perfectly concealed from the river by a stand of tall hemlocks. Jake nodded in appreciation. If it hadn't been for the chimney smoke, they might have passed within a hundred paces of the cabin without ever knowing it was there.

Jake watched for a while. There didn't seem to be any activity in the clearing around the cabin. He decided to slip down for a better look. Jake worked his way down the hillside and up through the grove of trees.

As he got closer, Jake noticed other details: in the clearing was a square-hewn log house, built into the side of the hills, its roof heavy with snow, a large set of elk antlers pegged up over the doorway. Under the eves of the roof, half-covered with snow,

lay a birchbark canoe.

Then Jake noticed something else, something curious: tied to a post driven into the snow by the doorway were three long ropes, each leading to a different spot in the clearing. One led to a small, sturdily-built shed, another to a woodpile under a grove of trees, and a third to a place at the far edge of the clearing where the snow was dirty with garbage and waste.

At first, Jake thought these might be be lines for hanging wet clothing. But he discarded that idea, they were too close to the ground. Then it came to him: these were handlines, maybe to be used in a storm, to guide a person around the clearing.

But before he could form any other theories, the cabin door creaked open and tall figure stepped out. He was dressed in hide clothing, like a trapper might wear, with one strange addition: he was wearing an large cloth blindfold. He groped around like a blind man. Jake watched him for a while as he worked his way down the hand-line toward the firewood pile.

Jake decided to take the direct approach. He stood up and shouted out a greeting, filling the clearing with his voice.

"Ho there fella!" he shouted, "Kin ya share yer fire with a poor traveler?"

The blindfolded man dropped down in the snow and whirled in Jake's direction. Jake saw a gleam of metal in the fading light. Then a deafening explosion filled the tiny clearing.

At the same instant, a heavy chunk of wood, torn from a nearby tree, struck Jake hard on the side of the head, making his ears ring. When Jake looked again, the blindfolded man was crouched in the snow with smoke curling from the barrel of his flintlock pistol.

Chapter Five

Jake skittered back behind a tree and cocked back the hammer on his rifle. He peered back into the clearing. He could see now that the blind man had drawn a pistol from his belt and had fired off a wild shot in Jake's direction, hoping to hit something.

"Don't mean any harm, fella." Jake shouted, "I was just passing through and thought you might like some company. Look, I know you only got one shot there. And I kin see that ya might be a bit skittish. If ya don't want any company, I'll just move along."

"No!" the man shouted back. "I haven't seen a human for two months. Fact is, I haven't seen anything for maybe a week. I didn't mean to part your hair. I guess I am a little jumpy. Being alone in the darkness can do that to a man."

Jake cautiously rose and walked out into the clearing, keeping an eye on the man's hands. But Jake could see that he meant no harm.

"Yer blind ain't ya?" Jake asked, when he was within a few paces.

The man nodded, turning his face in the direction of Jake's voice. "Snowblind. I been in darkness these seven days. My eyes hurt me like all getout."

The old man nodded. "I know, I've had a touch of the snowblindness myself at times. That sun coming up bright off the snow just makes the eyes close down and quit workin'. But you did the right thing with that blindfold. You keep the light from her eyes and in a few more days and yer vision will come back good as ever."

"You think so?"

"Sure thing. I've seen it happen many a time. Anyway," Jake chuckled, "that was a pretty good shot fer a blind man, you about took my topknot off."

Jake reached out and gripped the man's hand.

"My name's Jake Logan," he said.

"It's good to hear another human voice, "the big man said, "My name's Rory Garvin."

They shook on it.

Just then, they heard a dog's bark down by the river.

Rory raised his head, "You got a dog?"

"Yep, I s'pose I do," Jake admitted, "Listen, I didn't give ya the whole story. I'm traveling with a porcupine-eatin' dog and a spunky girl, name of Maggie Callahan, from the settlements down south. You got room fer us to hunker down with you tonight?"

The big man smiled. "Come on in. I haven't had nothin' but the wind to talk to these two months. We'll sit up by the fire and thaw ourselves and make some jaw music."

"Sounds good, "Jake said. Then he looked down through the trees and saw Poordevil loping ahead in long strides, coming up to Rory and growling.

"It's all right, you dumb dog," Jake said, "this here is our inn-keeper fer the night."

Just then, Maggie trudged up into the clearing, hauling the toboggan behind her.

"I heard the shot," Maggie said, breathless, "and I hurried down here as quick as I could. I thought maybe you were in trouble."

Jake shook his head. "Naw, this young fella here was just showing me some blind shootin'. Maggie, meet Rory Garvin. He's a bit snowblinded now."

Maggie got out of her harness and came across the clearing to shake his hand, "Glad to meet you, Mr. Garvin. Say, have you got any tea?"

Rory nodded. "Yes, I have a little. I ration it out so's it'll last. But I can spare a cup or two for you and your friend. "

"No," Maggie said, "That's not what I meant. I'm not asking

for us. I know a remedy for snowblindness. We can use the tea
to make up some hot compresses and lay them over your eyes. "

"Well, that does sound soothin'. I swear, my eyeballs feel
like they been fried in hot fat. "

Jake gestured towards the sled.

"We got a toboggan of provisions here, where should we
stow it?"

Rory nodded. "You'll have to unload it and set your bags in
the smokehouse there. There's wolves up in these hills and
they'll eat anything that not locked up. Just let me get a load of
firewood here and I'll get us situated for the night."

"That's alright, fella, me and Maggie will get the firewood.
You just make yer way back up inta the cabin and we'll meet ya
there."

They did the small chores quickly. Maggie and Jake
unloaded their goods, stowed them, and secured the smokehouse
door. Jake drew the toboggan up under the eaves of the cabin,
placing it safe beside the canoe.

It was dark now and getting very cold. But inside the tiny
cabin, the fire glowed warmly. Jake, Maggie and Poordevil came
inside and the old man shoved the door shut against the wind.

Maggie's eyes rolled over the firelit walls. Hanging from the
rafters were trapping implements, hides and bundles of dried
corn and leathered beans.

Jake glanced around, setting his rifle in the corner and

stomping his feet on the dirt floor. Along the far wall was a bunk covered by a huge bearskin. A carefully-laid stone fireplace held a cheerful fire. The walls were covered with shelves upon shelves, everything neat and in its place.

They settled themselves by the fire. Maggie slipped out of her frozen clothing. She didn't have to worry about privacy, with Rory snowblind and Jake turning his back as he customarily did when they were changing clothing on the trail. Jake was old-fashioned that way.

The old man had brought in their blankets and extra clothing. The travelers changed into dry clothing and moccasins and poured themselves a hot cup of tea. Poordevil stretched out on the dirt floor, near the hearth. Rory rummaged around through a soiled bag and found the dog a huge bear's thighbone. Poordevil's eyes grew wide with delight as he carried it to his place and began toothing it.

"I can't tell you what a pain it is losin' yer sight," Rory said, "I spent the first couple days just looking for stuff. But I'm pretty well organized now. And cooking—why I just about burnt my hands up trying to get the hang of lighting and caring for a fire."

"Listen," Maggie suggested, "before it gets any later, let's get those compresses on your eyes, it'll take some of the pain away for you."

The big man told Maggie where to find the sack of tea and she mixed up a slurry of crumbled tea leaves and hot water.

Then she spooned the leaves out into a long strip of white cloth, folding it over several times.

"Lay back on that bunk," Maggie said. She bent over him and unwound the head-wraps. She could see that he was not a bad-looking fellow, although it was obvious he had been through a lot. His beard was long and shaggy, his hair fell to below his shoulders. She wondered what color his eyes were, closed so tightly against even the faint light of the fire.

"Now you tell me if this is too hot."

Then she laid the compresses over his bared eyelids.

Rory gave a sudden jerk.

"Too hot?" she asked.

"No, Miss Callahan, that feels fine. Just gave me a start there for a minute. How long do you think I should keep these on?"

"Long as you can. Just rest easy and let the remedy do its work. A day or two of this and your eyes should come back as

good as new."

Rory smiled. "Wisht I woulda known this trick days ago."

"Say, "Jake said, "I noticed yer smokehouse out there, you smoke up your own meat?"

Rory grinned. "Garvin-smoked bear hams are the specialty of the house. There's a haunch of it over there on the table. Cut yourself a slice."

Jake drew his knife and made for it.

"That smokehouse was the first thing I built when I moved here six years ago. I lived in a tent while I finished the cabin. Made my livin' the first few years here by huntin' bear, rendering the hat and smokin' the hams. Traded with the Seneca villages here on the river."

Jake poured himself another cup of tea. "You got along well with them?"

"Tolerably well. Until the war started. Then they got partnered up with the British and things fell apart. But I had a few good years up here anyway. I traded mostly with the band over at Buccaloons."

Maggie recognized the name of the ruined village along the Allegheny. Jake brought her a slice of the smoked bear meat and Maggie bit into it, letting the smoky mixture slid around on her tongue.

"This is the best smoked meat I've ever tasted," she said. "What's your secret?"

Rory smiled. "I use shagbark hickory chips. Every year, in the fall, I hang the meat up in that smokehouse, each ham hanging from the rafters in there, then I build a low smoky fire on the dirt floor. The smoke curls up around them hams and dried them out, preservin' them for the winter and givin' them that smoky taste. Of course, the bear huntin' isn't what it used to be."

Jake nodded. "No huntin' is. Once these farmers start movin' in, the game just disappears."

Maggie smiled. "I'll warn you, Mr. Garvin, don't get Jake going on the evils of civilization or we'll be up all night."

Garvin laughed. "Well, what's the point of havin' company if you can't stay up all night? Besides, I don't usually find someone what agrees with me that progress ain't all it's cracked up to be."

"Now ain't that the truth," Jake said, warming to the subject. But before he could continue, Maggie interrupted.

"Listen, I've already had this discussion hundreds of times. If you men don't mind, I'll go out and bring in a bag of wheat flour and make up some bread."

Rory's mouth twitched. "Real bread, risen bread?"

Jake nodded, "This is the Callahan bread, rises up light and airy, makes a man's mouth glad to chomp inta."

"I haven't had a taste of real bread in months. You got all the fixins?"

"Just like you've got your ham-smoking," Maggie said, "We

have sort of a specialty in our family."

She reached down into the neckline of her shirt and drew out a leather pouch, about the size of her fist, hung around her throat by a leather thong.

"I know you can't see it, but inside this pouch I carry around my neck is the most precious thing I own. It's the great Callahan Spook Yeast, passed down for seven generations by the women in our family."

"Spook Yeast? That's a new one on me. What's it do?"

"It's the sourdough starter to make the bread rise. Without this yeast, the bread would be as flat as a brick. It's simple: nothing but flour and water, left to ferment. The yeast creatures fly through the air and come down to make a home in the dough. "That's how the first Callahan bread got started, back in Ireland, years ago. The yeast creatures livin' in this dough can trace their lineage all the way back to Dublin, in one long, unbroken chain.

"I'll mix up some wheat dough and then add these yeasties to it, let it rise overnight. Then I'll knead it down in the morning and rise it again. I'll bake us up some loaves tomorrow and we'll have fresh bread by noontime.

"It was my Aunt Franny who taught me to bake and passed the Spook Yeast along to me. She always said that the yeasties are a livin' thing and that if you add them to your bread, the bread comes alive, too.

"I see you have a cast-iron kettle here. I can make an oven of that."

"Go right ahead, "Rory grinned. "Now, Jake, getting back to what you were sayin'. I think the main problem is that the peoples came over from Europe and they never stopped to consider that this was a new land, with new ways. They just wanted to make it just like the old country."

Jake slapped his buckskinned thigh. "Now that's just what I've been sayin' myself for years. Now you take the French, when they came over here, they weren't interested in farmin', they started trappin'."

"'Course, that's got its own problems, "Rory said, interrupting, "Thanks to the fur trade, the streams is just about trapped out now, the Indians all has guns and whiskey and all kindsa diseases—"

"That's just what I've been sayin' for years!" Jake said.

Maggie set to work on her bread dough, kneading it and listening to the men talk, letting the calming motion of rolling and kneading the floured dough take her back to who she was and where she came from.

That night, when the four inhabitants of the cabin turned in, it was cramped but comfortable. Maggie lay in her blankets on the floor by the hearth. The fire had burned down low now, bathing the interior of the cabin in reddish-golden light.

Maggie stared up at the rafters in the half-darkness. She inhaled the smells of the cabin—the wild fragrances of the bear and beaver and deer skins, the manly odor of the buckskinned men asleep nearby, the gamey smell of Poordevil, and the delectable scent of rising bread dough laced with the sharp, smoky aroma of the hams.

Maggie closed her eyes and drifted off. Outside, the wind blew hard, whipping the snow around.

Chapter Six

When Maggie rose the next morning, the dough was puffed up in the pan, light and airy and ready to bake. She rolled out of bed, with the men still asleep beside her, and laid some dry wood on the hardwood coals. Outside, she could hear the wind whipping around the cabin. She rose and, clutching her blanket, peered out through the door. A heavy snow had fallen the night before and now a storm was coming in, drifting the snow across the clearing, covering the rope lines Rory had set up.

Poordevil stretched himself and pulled himself up on all fours, wanting to go out. Maggie let him slip by her and out into the snow.

"Well," Maggie thought to herself, "Maybe we can stay holed up here for a while." She had to admit, she was enjoying the rest from the cold and the hardship of the trail.

When Maggie turned back to the fire, it was burning brightly.

Jake was coming around now, rubbing the sleep from his eyes. Rory shifted in his bearskins. "Nice to wake up to a warm fire," Garvin commented, "How'd you folks sleep?"

Maggie grinned, "Like bear in hibernation. "

Jake just growled.

Rory laughed. "Well, yes, it seemed like that a little at times. How's that bread coming?"

Maggie was kneeling by the fire now. "We'll wait until the fire's burned down to coals then I'll lay that dough into the oven, put the top on and put a shovelful of coals on the lid. Then we'll have fresh bread in a half hour."

Just as Maggie said, the bread was baked to perfection. Maggie, Jake and Rory sat down to a warm breakfast of steaming sourdough bread, dipped in melted bear fat, and hot spearmint tea, sweetened with maple syrup.

After they cleared away the breakfast things, Maggie put on her coat and brought in a load of firewood. Poordevil slipped in behind her.

"It's storming' out there," she said as she closed the door, "Mind if we stay until it let's up?"

Rory grinned. "Glad to have ya. Stay on a day 'er two if ya like. It would actually be a help to me until I get my eyes back. Besides, there's no sense fightin' the storm."

It occurred to Maggie that although Rory had given her many details about his own life, he had never asked her why she was out on the Allegheny in this bitter weather. True to the frontier custom, she knew it was considered bad manners to ask a traveler where they had come from and where they were going.

What a person left behind was their own business. Almost everybody on the frontier had left behind something they didn't want to talk about. And where a person was headed was their own business as well. But Maggie saw no harm in telling him.

"We can't stay long," Maggie remarked, "We've got a long way to go. We're headed up the Genesee into the Seneca country."

Rory gave a low whistle. "That's a long ways," he said, "you two must have a mighty good reason fer goin' that far in this kinda weather."

It was not a question, just a statement that might or might not receive an reply.

"I spec' we do," Jake said, "But this here's for Maggie to tell, if she wants to—"

"I don't mind."

Then the whole story came pouring out— Maggie told how she had been captured by the Seneca years before, how the warriors had carried her up north to Little Beard's Village, where she had been married off to a Seneca, how they had had a son, how she had lost her Little Hoot Owl and vowed to get him back.

Rory nodded. "I know what it's like to lose somethin'" ya love," he said," I lost a dog once. Now I hope you won't laugh at me—losing a dog can be almost as bad as losing a child."

"I'm not laughing," Maggie said.

"Well, you've told me yer story and now I'll tell ya mine, if ya won't think I'm too foolish."

"Tell away," Maggie said, "I assure you, we won't think you're foolish."

"Well," Rory began,"It was maybe five years ago, back before the war. That was when I first met Hank. I didn't think much of him when I first laid eyes on him. He was just a pup then, just a few weeks old.

"I was doin' some fur tradin' down in Buccaloons with an old Indian fella there who I called Pine Tree, cause he was tall and thin like a pine. Now, I have never in my life known a man with such a knowledge of dogs. Dog training, dog sickness, dog personalities, dog ways—he knew it all. And it was a good thing, because in them days they was as many dogs in the village as people. They just multiplied like crazy, the dogs, I mean.

"Pine Tree and I finished our tradin' business. Then he said he had a present for me. He called back into his cabin and out comes one of his young sons, carrying this lubbering, floppy-ear mongrel pup. He presents him to me like he's givin' me a sack of gold and says, 'This will be good dog.' Well, I had my doubts but I didn't want to offend Old Pine Tree, so I took the little fella, put him in the canoe and set off fer my cabin acrost the river.

"Well, that first night away from his mama that pup cried all night and I was on the verge of givin' him back. But there was somethin' in his eye, something about the way he looked at me that prevented me from doin' it. To tell you the truth, I think I was just lonely as could be and not havin' a wife or any white companions, I guess Pine Tree thought this dog might be the best thing for me.

"Well, he was right about that, I named him Hank and that dog and I spent every wakin' hour together from then on. Come to think of it, we spent every sleeping hour together too—he would just snuggle down in the bearskin right along with me.

"I think sleepin' in that bearskin, and gettin' the smell of that bear up his nose was what made him such a good bear huntin' dog. I 'member the very first time we took him out for bear. Old Pine Tree and I went out one fall after black bear and we took along some of his best dogs and we took Hank along too, even though he was a little young.

"And you never saw a dog take to bear huntin' like Hank. He had a nose that could follow a bear's scent through water, trees, across bare rock, anywhere that bear went, Hank's nose would go. That was when I started to get into bear huntin' serious. I got myself a big .60 caliber bear hunting rifle and Hank and I would set off fer days at a time in the fall. When the hunting was good we would go upriver, chase down a bear, shoot him, skin him and canoe him downstream.

"Then it'd be bear steaks and bear loins and bear brains fer dinner fer a solid week. Hank would get the pick of the the bear bones. I'd render up bear fat in big kettles on the fire outside the cabin and Old Pine Tree showed me how the Indians would use the claws and sinew even the entrails of the bear to make things fer around the cabin. But the most delicious part of the operation—and the thing Hank and I loved the best —was smoking the bear hams.

"We would take those hams and hang them up in the smokehouse and smoke em up dry with shagbark hickory chips on the fire. And those hams were like solid gold in trade up and down this river.

"Then, one year, during the fall hunt, we had a turn of bad luck. I was out by myself with Hank and we was twenty miles west of here, over in the swamp country. We had run bear all that first day but hadn't caught anything and we were restin' our bones that night by a fire in the woods when we heard a terrible scream up in the hills behind us. It was the first time either Hank or I had heard a mountain lion. I had heard tell of them before but I had never actually heard one myself. If you haven't heard it, it is one of the eeriest sounds in all of creation. Sounds like a cross between a winter wind and a woman in childbirth pain.

Terrible sound.

"Well, the scream starts gettin' closer and Hank, loyal as always, goes dashin' off into the woods to scare this thing off. I called after him, trying to keep him back, but he was just determined to run that thing off. I heard a terrible thrashing around in the bushes. Hank's yelps of pain were all mixed up with the panther's screams. I clutched up a torch from the fire and my horse pistol and went out into the thicket after them.

"I suppose the light from my torch scared that mountain lion off. But there was no sign of Hank. I finally located him, he was lying on his side on the thicket, his head and shoulders and paws just scratched to ribbons. I thought he was dead at first. But then he looked up at me and whined and I knew he still had a chance.

"I carried him back to the river and brought him down to Old Pine Tree in the village. The old man used hot comfrey leaves for the bandages and said Hank would heal from the wounds in time.

"But he said there was another problem. Some people said there was a woods-witch up in the swampy hills that was taken' on the shape of a panther and luring dogs out from their masters then attackin' em. And Old Pine Tree said that if a dog was scratched by one of them panthers, it was only a matter a time before that dog went crazy and and would start actin' out during the full moon time.

"Well, I watched Hank real careful after that and in a few

weeks his wounds healed and I figured he was all right.

"Then, one night, a strange thing happened. It was in early December and we still hadn't gotten any snow yet, but it was cold in the evenin's . I went out to the smokehouse that night to select a ham for our dinner. I used a little pine pitch torch to see my way. Hank and I opened the big hickory slat door like we always did. We kept that door barred because there are plenty animals would like to steal off those hams. And when we would open that door, the smell of those smoked hams rollin' out was enough to make a fella's mouth water.

"Anyway, I reached up —— Then I noticed—one of the hams was missing. I counted them again but, sure enough, there were only eleven. There should have been twelve hams because every bear I've ever seen has two ham on 'im."

"I said, 'Hank,what can this mean? What kinda animal has been in here? Sniff 'im out boy!'

"Hank sniffed around the door and all the way around the smokehouse but he couldn't seem to find anythin'. I had never known his nose to fail like that. I closed the door firm and latched it. The moon was shining real bright that night, full moon up in the sky. And I 'member my torch went out. But the moonlight was so bright I didn't need it to walk back to the cabin.

"That night, I sat up here by the fireplace and smoked my pipe and tried to think. I thought maybe I had just forgotten to count the hams or had lost one somewheres along the way. Then

I noticed that Hank was all atremblin' in his dreams. He yelped and as if something was passing over him, making him afeared.

"Well, I checked the next morning and even though the smokehouse door was locked, another bear ham was missin! I was furious! I was down to ten hams for the winter. I called Hank and he sniffed around, but he seemed dull and listless, like he'd been up all the night.

"Again, that night, he had those trembly dreams. Then I remembered an old trick that Pine Tree had showed me one time. He said it was a sure-fire way to figure out what a dog is dreamin'. I thought it was worth a try.

"As Hank was asleep on the floor, I crept over to my shelf and took down a piece of soft canvas cloth. Careful not to wake Hank, I laid that cloth over his sleeping eyes and ears and nose and left it there until he quit shiftin' around. Then I pulled that canvas up off him and laying on my own bed, I laid that cloth over my own face.

"Sure enough, I fell asleep and in that sleep, I started dreamin'. I started dreamin' I was a dog." Maggie and Jake sat quietly, staring into the fire.

"Yer not going to think I'm foolish if I go on?" Rory asked.

"No," Maggie said, "not at all, go on..."

Chapter Seven

"Well," Rory said, "I know this is a little hard to believe, but I swear it's true. I started dreamin' I was a dog. In fact, I started dreamin' I was Hank, the dog.

"I saw myself waking up in Hank's body there on the cabin floor, he looked over and there was me, Rory Garvin, layin' in the bed asleep.

"Hank crept silent acrost the floor, careful not to wake me. With his paw, he pushed open the door and stepped out into the moonlight. Hank headed straight for the smokehouse.

"He leaped on a stump nearby and from the stump up onto the roof of the smokehouse. Placing his paws on either side of the smoke hole, he reached down into the smokehouse and plucked one of those hams off the peg on the rafters. Now I had a little trap door on the chimney top to keep squirrels out, but he just pushed that aside with his nose then let it fall back down into place.

"With that bear ham in his teeth, Hank jumped down off the

roof of the smokehouse and ran back into the woods for a few hundred paces. There he stopped and feasted on that ham. But he couldn't finish the whole thing. And, like a dog will do, he dug a hole there in the hillside and buried that hambone.

"Then he trotted back to the clearing, slipped in the door, pushed it closed with his nose, and laid down on the floor and fell asleep as if nothing had happened.

"Now, that was the dream I had. The next morning when I opened my eyes, I snatched that piece of cloth off my face and without so much as a glance at Hank, I made straight for that smokehouse.

"Sure enough, another ham was missin!

"I walked around to the back of the smokehouse and found a set of tracks going back into the woods. I started followin' 'em. But after a while I didn't need to follow the tracks, because every rock and every tree was clear, just like it was in my dream. Soon I was standin' beside that big hemlock tree. I knew right where to dig. And I came up with what I hoped I wouldn't find—three half-eaten bear hams.

"I stormed back to the cabin and shook those hambones at Hank, all the while shoutin', 'Hank! What's the meanin' of this? I thought you and I were partners! You're nothin' but a common thief!'

"Well, poor Hank, he cowered and whined and crept forward as if he was beggin' my forgiveness. But I wasn't havin' any of it. I grabbed a piece of rope and tied it tight around Hank's neck, led him down to the canoe and took him acrost to Old Pine Tree, told him the whole story.

"Pine Tree sat there by his fire, smokin' his clay pipe and lookin' at Hank.

" 'Looks like the full-moon sickness to me,' he said.

"Then he explained. Folks said that if a dog got so much as a scratch from one of them nightcats, they would go moon-struck. The full moon illness would hit them hard, makin' 'em act crazy. But the rest of the time they'd act normal.

"'Well,' I told Pine Tree,' I can't have a dog that steals from me, full moon or not.'

"Pine tree took the pipe from his mouth and nodded. 'I understand. He just steals? He hasn't bit you or tried to ruin anything in the cabin?'

"I shook my head. 'No. But, even so, I can't keep a dog that steals from me.'

"Pine Tree reached out and rubbed Hank on the head.

" 'I'll keep him with me,' the old man said, 'I'll have the boys pen him up during the moon-time so's he doesn't cause any trouble.'

"I nodded and handed the rope over to him. Hank was watching' every move I made, knowing that somethin' peculiar was happenin'. When I stood up to go, Hank stood up too, as if to follow me, but the old man held him firm by the rope. I walked out of the cabin without so much as backward look.

"As I was gettin' in my canoe, I heard Hank bark. I could see that Old Pine Tree had him tied up to the sapling by the cabin door. Hank struggled against the rope but couldn't pull free. In all of his life Hank had never known ropes or collars or leashes. He was a free dog.

"When Hank saw that I was pushin' off from shore and leavin' him behind, he put his muzzle in the air and gave out the longest, most lonesome moan I have ever heard. It was hard to paddle away that day and leave him, but I didn't see any other way, because you can't keep a dog that steals from ya.

"Well, I paddled back to the cabin and checked the smokehouse. The hams were safe. Then I set about fixin' my dinner. But the old cabin didn't seem the same without Hank. I was so used to him doggin' my steps that it felt like I had gone and lost my shadow.

"I wanted Hank back, sure enough. But I had given him away and I couldn't take him back, that woulda been an insult to Pine Tree. So I let things be.

"It got kinda difficult to visit the village after that because they just let Hank run free and except fer his few days a month when they kept him penned up, he was all right. Every time I'd come down to the village he's come running up to me leaping round and lickin' me. It was enough to break a man's heart because both he and I knew that no matter how many masters he had, he and I would always be partners. So I stayed away from the village a fair amount after that. It was just too heart-breakin' fer both of us.

"The boys told me that Hank would meet the canoes that came in and every canoe that came in he would look at and sniff, hoping I would be on it. And sometimes, at night, he would run up and down the riverbank, barking and howling trying to call me out out my cabin. But I refused to have anything to do with him. I figured as long as there was a river between him and me, I wouldn't be bothered by him. He wasn't a very good swimmer and even if he was, the current was pretty strong there and Hank knew better than to attempt swimmin' acrost.

"Then one day, Pine Trees' sons paddled over to get a load of smoked hams for trade. I shouldn't have sent those hams over to the village. I just wasn't thinkin' about what effect them hams would have on Hank.

"When the boys brought them hams back inta the village, it just drove Hank crazy. A few of the boys told me about it later. When the boys pulled up in that canoe, They said Hank came out like he always did and sniffed around them as they unloaded. But when he caught a scent of those Garvin-smoked hams, the poor dog just went crazy.

"He gave out a terrible howl and dashed into the river, swimming hard and strong upstream, swimming against the current, trying to cross over and make it up to my cabin. The boys yelled after him and tried to stop him. But it was too late. He got caught in a big eddy in the center of the river and it drug him down.

"The boys and I searched downstream for miles the next morning. But we never found the body. I suppose he was drowned, trying to swim back to me. But sometimes I like to think that maybe he got washed ashore somewheres downstream and that maybe he's still alive somewhere, going through his monthly cycle of craziness.

"And you've never heard from him since?" Jake asked.

"No, I haven't. I'll admit that sometimes I like to think that he'll make it back to me. Sometimes I imagine that I'll be settin' here some day and I'll look up and there'll be Hank, running up through the clearin', with his tongue hanging out and his ears flopping and that twinkly look in his eye."

Rory was silent for a few moments.

"I never shoulda given him away," the big man whispered. "I shoulda forgiven him like he woulda me, if he woulda been the man and I woulda been the dog. He was my dog."

Maggie laid a comforting hand on Rory's shoulder.

"I understand Rory. I hope yer dog comes back some day."

Maggie did understand. She understood what it was to hope against hope that the thing you've lost will someday make it back to you.

Chapter Eight

A storm came up the next morning, not a full-fledged storm, but enough to give Maggie and Jake an excuse for staying on at Rory's place for a day or two. It was good to be in out of the wind. And the combination of Maggie's bread and Rory's smoked hams allowed them to regain some of their strength.

Jake had found a fresh ear for his bear stories. Rory found someone to commiserate with about the war and the Indians and the decline of the fur trade.

At last, the storm moved on and Maggie and Jake knew it was time for them to move on as well. Before they left, Maggie had attempted to remove the blindfold across Rory's eyes, but the light was still too strong. Both Jake and Maggie felt bad about leaving him in darkness but he assured them he would be all right.

"I don't mean to hold you back on my account," Rory told them, "I've enjoyed yer company. Stop off at the smokehouse on your way out and pick out a smoked ham to take on the trail with ya. Feel free to stop in on your way back downriver."

Then, more quietly, he said to Maggie, "I hope you find yer boy."

"Thanks, Rory. I hope you find your dog."

Then it was time to go. Jake had the sled packed and had brought their snowshoes out into the clearing before the cabin. Rory stood in the doorway, feeling the winter sunlight on his face.

"Clear day," he remarked, "you watch out for snowblindness. Make yourself some birchbark goggles if ya have to."

"Surely will," Jake said. He slipped into the toboggan harness. "Good luck to ya, Garvin."

Then they set off toward the river trail. Maggie called Poordevil and he trotted ahead. It was astonishing how much their bodies had softened in just three days away from the trail. Within an hour, Maggie's leg muscles were begging for relief. The constant shushing of the snowshoes lulled her into the monotony of travel. What's more, she now felt open to the cold. Even though they were walking steadily, Maggie couldn't seem to get warm. Although he didn't complain, Maggie knew that Jake was feeling the strain as well. They moved slowly, camping early that night.

It was strange to walk upriver, into the fresh and silent snow, without the cabin smells and comforts around them. It was strange to camp at night, under the open sky, shivering in their blankets in the snow.

In time, they fell back into the routine of travel and were soon making fifteen miles a day, just as they had on the first leg of the journey.

When Maggie and Jake reached the upper waters of the Allegheny, they found the old Seneca Warrior's Trail which took them up along Oil Creek and into the Seneca Country. After three days of flatland travel, they met up with the Genesee River and followed that waterway north, into even colder weather.

They knew they were not alone now. Now and then, they saw the smoke of refugee bands camped along the river and once or twice they even heard the barks of camp dogs. But they skirted around the ragged villages and headed further north.

Things began to look familiar to Maggie when they reached the Great Genesee Gorge. There they climbed the great rocky cliffs that rose above the river. One cold afternoon, Maggie stood on the bluff overlooking the great falls. Even the great cold couldn't stop these falls. The water was moving at a terrifying rate over the edge of the precipice, filling the gorge with a thunderous roar as the water plunged into an icy pool a hundred feet below.

Maggie remembered how the warriors had brought her this way, two summers before, leading her along the war trail by a

rawhide cord, noosed around her neck. To Maggie, that seemed a long time ago. A lot of water had gone over the falls since then.

At last, on the afternoon of their twenty-first day of walking, Maggie and Jake followed the winding river into the great Genesee valley. It was quiet, deserted, no birds in the trees, even the wind wasn't blowing.

In memory, Maggie could see Little Beard's Village as it had been during her captivity. In the warm months, when everything was green and growing, the village was like a jewel set in the center of the broad flat valley. She could still see the well-kept log cabins, the fruit trees and the gardens, the lush fields and grasslands. But she knew none of that would be there. It was winter now. And besides, Sullivan had burnt it all.

Still, Maggie half-expected the village to be there. She expected to see the houses repaired, to see the cabins snug and warmly lit, with firewood stacked neatly by the doorways and children playing in the deep snow.

But none of this prepared her for the sight of the ruins of Little Beard's Village in winter.

Maggie and Jake crossed the frozen Genesee and walked up into the trees that ringed the town. Maggie was pulling the toboggan. She stopped and stood in her harness, staring.

"God Amighty," she said.

What she saw was the blackened skeleton of the place she

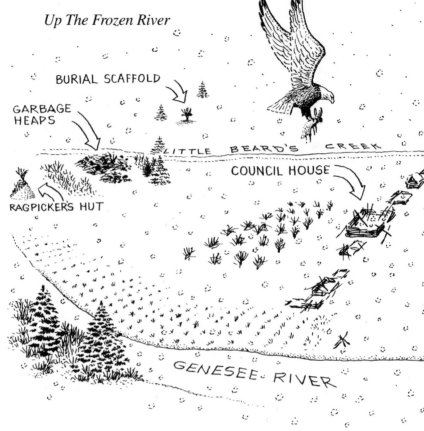

BURIAL SCAFFOLD

GARBAGE
HEAPS

RAGPICKER'S HUT

LITTLE BEARD'S CREEK

COUNCIL HOUSE

GENESEE RIVER

had known, covered in drifted snow.

"God Amighty, Jake," she whispered again, "It's all strange and ghosty up here."

And it was. As Maggie walked down what had once been the main road, each ruined house and yard held some small landmark of memory, calling back a person or a thing that had once been there.

Further down, across the ice-choked tributary of Little Beard's Creek, Maggie recognized the ruins of the cabin where she and her companion Frenchgirl had raised their babies and cooked for their husbands. Half the roof was caved in.

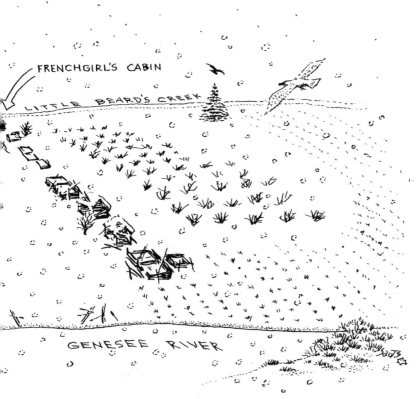

FRENCHGIRL'S CABIN

LITTLE BEARD'S CREEK

GENESEE RIVER

Maggie walked ahead, watching the ghosts of memory rise from the fields and the buildings.

"We best find a cabin to hole up in," Jake suggested. "This one here don't look too bad. Gimme that sled and I'll pull it inside."

Maggie obeyed numbly, as her eyes cast up and down the main road, watching the ghosts of memory rising from the buildings and the fields.

Then Maggie saw something that tugged at her even more strongly: Out across the windswept cornfield, standing stark and alone, was Firefly's tree. On the wooden scaffold in the branches, Maggie could see the bundle of bones that had once been her husband.

"Jake," she said softly, "I have to go down there. You keep the dog here with you."

"Don't ya wanta warm yerself by a fire first, get a cup of tea in ya?"

"No," Maggie said absently, "gotta go."

Like a woman in a trace, Maggie left the cluster of buildings and walked out into the fields, snowshoeing through the deep drifts.

At last, she was there. Removing one of her mittens, Maggie placed her hand against the rough bark of the tree and tilted her head back, looking up at the bundle of cloth on the scaffold.

"Don't worry," she whispered to Firefly, "I'll find the boy."

Then Maggie leaned forward and, placing her forehead against the tree, she closed her eyes and wept.

When Maggie opened her eyes, her vision was blurred with cold and emotion. She wiped the tears away with the back of her mitten. Then Maggie's eyes fell on something black in the snow: the dead embers of a freshly kindled fire.

Maggie glanced around.

"Someone is here. Someone is making the fire for Firefly."

Maggie searched the ground for tracks. There was nothing distinct, just a twin set of holes in the snow, leading down toward the garbage heaps, where the Ragpicker lived.

Then, raising her eyes, Maggie caught a glimpse of motion down by the garbage heaps. There, in the gathering darkness, a hunched-over figure, wrapped in a ragged black blanket, was poking through the refuse heap with a stick.

Maggie slipped behind the tree. A tingling shot up her spine. She had wanted to find the Ragpicker, yes. But she had not expected to meet up with her so soon.

A part of her shrunk back behind the tree. She debated going back to the cabin for Jake and Poordevil. But, no, she would go ahead. She would meet the old woman and do whatever had to be done to get her boy back.

As Maggie stepped off in the deep snow, she felt for her hatchet, which hung in it's leather scabbard at her belt. If she needed a weapon, she knew her short-handled axe could be deadly if it came to a physical struggle.

The snow was soft and fine and she walked quietly. The woman did not notice her.

When Maggie was a dozen paces away, the ragged figure straightened and whirled to face her.

Maggie stepped back in astonishment.

"It's you!" she breathed.

At the sound of her voice, the ragged one ran a dozen steps toward her and encircled Maggie in her arms. As Maggie peered into the dirty face before her, she knew this woman for who she was—her faithful companion from her captive days—

Frenchgirl.

"Redwing, can it really be you?"

It was strange for Maggie to hear her Seneca name again.

"Yes, of course," Maggie said, holding her friend out at arm's length, looking into her care-worn face, "it's me."

Frenchgirl sighed. "You frightened me. When I first saw you, I thought you might be a ghost."

Maggie nodded. "I understand. This place is full of ghosts—ghosts of memory."

"More than you know," Frenchgirl said sadly.

"Are you alone?"

"Yes, alone."

"Where are Cornstalk and the Little Rabbit and the others?"

Frenchgirl was silent. Maggie could feel her friend's shoulders trembling.

Then she knew. "They are dead, aren't they?"

Frenchgirl nodded, tears welling up in her eyes.

Maggie held her friend tightly. "You can tell me about it later. But for now, I must ask you: Have you seen Hoot Owl or the Ragpicker?"

Frenchgirl shook her head. "They are not here. I have been here for ten days and I haven't seen anything moving, nothing but the wolves and the wind. Forgive me, Redwing, but—I must ask—Do you have anything to eat? I am very hungry."

"Of course, I have a little food up in the village. I'm

traveling with a friend, an old man who is a good hunter and—"

"You have traveled all this way, from the Allegheny? But why?"

"We can talk later. For now, let's get in out of the cold and get you a bowl of hot venison soup."

Frenchgirl nodded. "I have been camped out in the ruins of our old cabin. Most of the roof is still there and I have blocked off the holes in the walls with boards. It will be good to sit by our own fire again, eh?"

It was almost dark now. The two friends turned and stumbled up through the deep snow, up out of the fields and into the village where Frenchgirl angled off towards the cabin while Maggie snowshoed down to the cabin where Jake was just laying up a fire in the drafty chimney.

"Jake!" she hollered in through the doorway, "Frenchgirl is here! I met her down by the dumps. We can drag the sled down to her cabin and set up there."

Jake said, "Good enough. How's yer friend?"

"She's about starved from what I can see. I hope you don't mind, I offered her some of our rations. You can take her portion out of my share if you want."

The old man came out into the failing light and slipped into the toboggan harness, "Don't you worry 'bout that. Me and Poordevil will set out tomorrow mornin' and bring us in some fresh meat fer the stewpot."

By the time Maggie, Jake and Poordevil had reached Frenchgirl's cabin, the young woman had a brisk fire going in the hearth. Maggie could see the light coming from the holes in the walls and roof.

Poordevil pushed his way in through the door and Frenchgirl let out a terrified scream. Poordevil knocked her down and was all over her, licking her face and sniffing her hair.

"It's all right," Maggie said, "He's just friendly."

Frenchgirl laughed. It was the laugh Maggie remembered from their times together, so long ago. "No worries," Frenchgirl said. "I thought he was a wolf."

"More like wolf-bait," Jake said, stepping through the doorway, "My name's Jake Logan and if yer a friend of Maggie's you're sure enough a friend of mine. Now let me pull this sled inside and we'll get a stewpot on that fire of yers."

Maggie reached into her beltpouch and pulled out a stick of dried jerky.

"Here," she said, "chew on this until we can get some real food going."

Frenchgirl took the strip of meat and made a meal of it.

"I'll make us up some sassafras tea," Maggie was saying, "and I have enough flour for some Callahan biscuits. Remember the biscuits I used to tell you about? And—Oh yes!—I almost forgot!—We've got some smoked bear's meat here—that'll bring back your strength."

Frenchgirl sunk down on the dirt floor by the fire and chewed on her strip of jerky, watching as Maggie and Jake bustled about, getting a meal on the fire.

It took forever for the tea water to boil and for the stewpot to heat. But at last they ladled the steaming food out into bowls and poured mugs of hot tea all around. Jake laid out some marrow bones Rory had given them for Poordevil. Then the four settled down to the serious business of eating. No time for talking now. They were eating what Maggie knew was the last of their thin rations. It wasn't a feast exactly, but it felt like it.

At last, when they had finished, Maggie asked, "What happened that day—the day Sullivan came? I lost track of you in all the noise and confusion."

Frenchgirl licked the venison broth from her lips. "I lost track of you as well. I was with the clan women when the call came in, we didn't have time to pack anything. I just snatched up my little girl and wrapped her in a blanket. We ran for the woods and hid the best we could. The soldiers did not come after us.

"We hid out there, with our children for a long time. Then we heard the soldiers coming in, with their music playing. We saw the dust clouds raised by their horses. Then we saw other clouds—clouds of smoke— and we knew that they were burning the village.

"The soldiers took our village without a fight. Redwing, how many soldiers did this General Sullivan have?

Jake spoke up, "I heared he had an army of 1500 men. They destroyed 'bout forty villages on the whole campaign."

Frenchgirl nodded. "I heard later that the British and our warriors tried to mount a defense but that it made no sense, so they abandoned the valley. The British told us we could come to Fort Niagara, five days march to the north, and we could winter there with them. They said they would give us shelter and food and blankets. But Redwing, they lied.

"At Niagara, there were not enough provisions for the British themselves. So we were forced to live on short rations of our own corn, corn reaped from Seneca fields and stored at the fort. And Redwing—it was the coldest place I have ever been. We built bark huts on the lakeshore around the fort. The wind coming in off that lake carried cold air from the North and froze us. Many people died of disease and cold. Then the British poisoned our corn."

"They did what?"

"They put poison in the corn they gave us. That is how my husband died. It was a ruthless way of cutting down on the number of hungry mouths to feed.

"I left Cornstalk up in the land of frozen winds and went away from that place with a few other women. We took our babies and left that evil place. We were determined to make it back here and spend the winter in our own valley. But that was a foolish plan. Traveling the winter trail was worse than staying at the fort.

Frenchgirl stared into the fire. "I woke one morning in our trail camp and saw that I was the only one alive. All of my companions—" and here her voice began to break—"all of my trusted companions, women I have know since I was a girl, and our young children too—they were frozen solid in their blankets. I don't know why I am still alive. I left my little Rabbit, wrapped in blanket, up in the crook of a cedar tree. If I am still alive in the spring I will go back and bury her."

Maggie stared into the fire. There was nothing to say. Frenchgirl's grief lay heavy in the room. Jake quietly poured a cup of tea and passed it to Frenchgirl.

"Thank you," she said quietly.

They drank the tea until it was gone and then they rolled up in their blankets by the fire. Maggie spread her blanket down on the dirt floor beside her friend and gathered her up in her arms. It was like holding a small, frail child. Maggie lay awake for a while, looking at the dirt-streaked face of her friend. She was thin now, but still lovely. But when Maggie gathered her body up in the blankets, she was astonished at how thin her friend had become.

Chapter Nine

When Maggie woke the next morning, Jake and Poordevil had already left for the hunt. Maggie was determined to make her way down to the Ragpicker's hut and see if she could find any clues which would lead her back to her boy. She knew she should have waited for the old man and the dog to return, but she was impatient. The thought that her boy might be somewhere nearby, huddled in the arms of the old woman, was too powerful.

Before Maggie left for the hut, she mixed up a wooden bowl of flour and starter and set it by the fire to rise. She planned to make biscuits for Frenchgirl as soon as she returned.

When Maggie went out, her feet naturally lead her to the path which took her down to the Ragpicker's hut. Even if she found nothing in the thicket, she could haul back the day's firewood. Everything was covered in snow there, the hut was hidden under many feet of snow, just the very top of the dome peeking out.

Maggie couldn't shake off the idea that the Ragpicker and Hoot Owl were somewhere nearby. But what Frenchgirl had said was true, there were no human tracks going into the thicket and none coming out. There were no signs of fire-making or wood gathering or watercarrying or any of the other signs of camp life.

Maggie walked for an hour through the thicket, looking and listening, picking up firewood as she went. At last there was no point in looking anymore. Whatever had happened here was covered by snow.

But she did see something which sent a chill down her spine. An owl, circling and lighting on tree branch nearby, looked down at her as if it knew something that she didn't. Maggie stood for a long time watching the owl, then collected her firewood and headed back.

When she came back through the cabin door, Maggie noticed that the dough rising by the fire was missing. She asked Frenchgirl what had happened to it.

Her friend gave an embarrassed laugh, "I ate it."

"You ate it raw? That isn't good for your stomach."

"I know," Frenchgirl admitted, "my stomach knew that too, I felt sick and I went out and tossed it out into the snow."

Maggie was annoyed. "That is a waste of food." But then she brightened, "All right, I'll rise some more. But we only have enough for one more batch of bread, with a little flour left over. We have to be very careful not to waste anything."

"I understand," Frenchgirl said grimly.

They made a soup that night with the last of Maggie's dried beans and jerked venison.

Jake and Poordevil came back from hunting at mid-morning.

"Nuthin' movin' out there, I spec we'll have to go further up inta the woods to get us some game."

The men used to go elk hunting up into the cedar swamps a day's travel north," Maggie offered. She remembered the swamp well. She had once been lost up there.

"Well," Jake said, "Me and Poordevil, we'll set out tonight and head up there fer a few days, bring us back enough meat to get us through 'til spring."

That afternoon Frenchgirl and Maggie sat and talked and she seemed to be her old self. Maggie told about her trek downriver and about their winter walk back upstream.

Maggie went out that night to light the fire by Firefly's tree. But when she came back, Frenchgirl was huddled in her blankets, asleep.

In the morning, Jake prepared for the hunt. He loaded the toboggan with a few provisions.

"I'll take this dog along," Jake commented. Poordevil pranced about in the snow, as if he was anxious to be on the trail once again.

Maggie said goodbye to them at the cabin door.

"Good huntin' to you, Jake. Get us something big and meaty. Poordevil, you take good care of 'im."

"He's just a travelin' nose, is all he is." Jake said. Then he pulled the shoulder harness on, snatched up his rifle and set out, headed north, up the Genssee trail.

Maggie stood in the doorway of the cabin for a long time, watching the old man and the dog disappear.

"Godspeed to ya," she whispered, knowing that their lives depended upon the luck of the hunter.

Maggie went about her morning tasks. She woke Frenchgirl and helped her friend wash herself with a bowl of tepid water and a rag. Then she set out for her morning errand, continuing the ever more difficult search for firewood. She would also collect clean snow to melt for drinking water.

In an hour, she was back at the cabin. But when she came through the door, she was shocked at what she saw.

Frenchgirl was sitting on the cabin floor with the last of the flour bag open before her, stuffing dried flour into her mouth with both hands and weeping. Her chest and hands and face were dusted with flour and the dirt floor around her was sprinkled with the last of the precious grain.

Frenchgirl looked up, her eyes red with tears, and muttered through a full mouth, "I'm sorry, Redwing. I was just so hungry."

Maggie felt a great anger rising within her.

"Have you lost your senses?" she shouted, "That's the last of our food!"

Frenchgirl began to weep.

"I know," she sobbed, "I knew it was wrong but I did it anyway. I have a wanting creature inside of me, this thing that wants to eat.

"It whispers in my ear, 'Here is food. You can have it. All you need to do is take it and it is yours.'

"I resisted as long as I could. But this morning, the voice was too loud. I had to do it."

Maggie's anger evaporated.

"I understand," she said.

Maggie knew what it was to be hungry and afraid, driven on by voices of starvation's ghosts, voices that tempted and taunted until they got their way.

She thought about all the times when Frenchgirl has been strong and sure and capable, back when Maggie had first come among the Seneca and been given into Frenchgirl's care. Now it was Maggie's turn to care for her friend.

"There is nothing to eat now," Frenchgirl sobbed. "What will we live on until spring? "

Maggie smiled, "We will live on the same thing I lived on when I was a captive in this village. We will live on companionship.

"Frenchgirl, I had wanting creature inside of me then, it wanted love and freedom and you gave me that. That was what kept me alive. And now, I would rather have your companionship in this hard time than all the flour and cornmeal in the colonies."

Frenchgirl smiled. "Thank you, Redwing."

Maggie reached down and used the index finger of her right hand to wipe a tear from Frenchgirl's flour-dusted cheek. And, for no reason that was clear to her, Maggie put her teary finger into her mouth. She tasted the saltiness of Frenchgirl's tears and the graininess of the wheat flour. She rolled the taste around on her tongue, knowing that it might be the last thing she would get to eat for a long, long time.

When Maggie went out for firewood the next morning, she was glad she had nothing to guard. Their food was gone now. She wracked her brain, trying to devise some way of wresting food from the cruel, snow-covered land. Maggie had tried fishing through the ice in the river. She had tried setting snares for rabbits in the deep snow. But her skill and her luck were poorly matched and she caught nothing. In desperation, she had searched the abandoned cabins and the garbage heaps for food. But there was nothing but a great emptiness.

This left the bark on the trees as their last choice. Walking to a stand of maple trees, Maggie drew her knife and began shaving the bark into long strips. They would boil this pulpy, paperly substance in pots to soften it and then they would eat as much as their stomachs would allow. It would at least give them the illusion that they were eating.

Each morning, Maggie passed through the Ragpicker's old camp and each evening she went out to light the fire at Firefly's tree. In between, she did her best to keep her friend alive and to think of how they would live out the next 30 days.

One afternoon, when Maggie came back from collecting maple bark, Frenchgirl greeted her with a big grin.

"Redwing, throw out that bark. I have something special for our dinner tonight," she announced.

Maggie's face lit up. "You found us something to eat?"

Frenchgirl nodded. "I have a real treat for us—Bag soup!"

Maggie laughed. It was the first time she had laughed in days.

"Yes. Come and sit down by the fire. I'll make you up a bowl."

Maggie took off her coat and sat on the ground by the fire. Frenchgirl went to a pot hanging over the flames and ladled a strange-smelling liquid out into a wood bowl, handing it to Maggie. Maggie sniffed the steam rising off of the bowl.

Maggie lifted the wooden bowl to her lips and took a sip. She swished the broth around in her mouth.

"What do you think?" Frenchgirl asked.

Maggie made a face. "It tastes like canvas."

"Well, of course it does. This is canvas bag soup. I made it by boiling up the food bags. I thought there might be a little food clinging to the seams. Now tell me, what do you really think of it?"

"It's horrible," Maggie said honestly.

Frenchgirl smiled. "No, Redwing, you have to use your imagination. This is the sort of soup that is only served once a year, at some great feast.

"Close your eyes," Frenchgirl commanded.

Maggie sat with her eyes closed, the bowl of strange soup steaming on her lap.

"Now," Frenchgirl said, "remember the smell of sizzling venison steaks, with crisp carrots and potatoes and onions."

Maggie began licking her lips.

"Ah," Maggie sighed, "those onions..."

"And now, take another sip and taste the peppercorns and the plump black beans and the hickory nuts..."

Frenchgirl went on to describe the best foods her imagination could conjure up and Maggie sat with eyes closed, sipping the weak broth and nodding. She was so taken by Frenchgirl's descriptions that it almost seemed, for a moment, that she was sipping some rich stew, some concoction of earthy delights. At last she opened her eyes. She had finished her bowl.

"More?" Frenchgirl inquired.

"Only if you will join me," Maggie said politely.

Frenchgirl brought them two steaming bowls.

Maggie grinned. "I wonder if this is what they mean at a church social when they tell you to bring a bag lunch?"

Both women burst out laughing.

"No," Frenchgirl said, "this is what the British mean when they say they are going to sack a city."

They collapsed in laughter.

"This is not funny," Maggie said soberly. Then they both burst out in laughter, rolling on the floor. They laughed for an hour about absolutely nothing. Which was exactly what was needed at the time.

The next morning Frenchgirl couldn't rise from her blankets, she was simply too weak.

"Don't leave me," Maggie said simply.

Frenchgirl swallowed hard. "Thirty days is a very long time, Redwing."

"It is only 28 now," Maggie answered.

Frenchgirl shook her head. "It may be 35, it may be 40, "she said slowly. Then she said, "I want to go out to Firefly's tree."

Maggie tried to pretend that she didn't know what Frenchgirl was talking about. "But you shouldn't go out in the wind," she protested, "I don't think you can walk."

Frenchgirl was adamant. "If I can't walk, you will carry me."

"Listen," Maggie said urgently, "I have an idea. There are people downstream. I'll travel down there and see if I can beg some food from them."

Frenchgirl shook her head. "No, Redwing. I have seen you struggle to bring in the firewood each day. You would die of exhaustion within a few miles. Take me out to the tree now."

"But Jake and Poordevil will be back in a day or two with fresh meat. We can live."

"You don't understand, Redwing," Frenchgirl said. Her voice was only a hoarse whisper.

"What is there to live for?" she asked. "I know how this war will end. And I know that we will be strangers in our own land when it does. Without the land, we are nothing. All the Seneca will be forced to move further west, to accept the hospitality of other tribes. That is no way for a Seneca woman to live."

"No," Maggie said, "you won't have to do that."

She was, at last, saying something that she had thought about for a long time.

"I can take you back to Kittanning with me."

Frenchgirl laughed sadly. "They would not welcome a Seneca there."

"But you could pass for White. No one would have to know you were a Seneca."

Frenchgirl's eyes flashed with anger. "I do not wish to pass for a White! And I certainly would not wish to go back to a brutal world like yours, where the women are treated as cattle owned by their men."

"It's not so bad—"

"Redwing, look at me. Didn't you learn anything when you lived among us? Didn't you learn what it was to be a free woman?"

"But I was a captive!"

"You were free, Redwing, you were free for the first time in your life. I know you understand this."

Maggie dropped her eyes. "Yes," she said quietly, "It's true. I can't picture going back to being some settler's wife, barefoot and pregnant, with a gaggle of geese and babies to feed."

Frenchgirl nodded. "Then I hope you will understand why it is best for me to go to the spirit world now."

There was something in the tone of her friend's voice which compelled Maggie to do as she was asked.

Maggie pulled her friend's moccasins on her feet and tied the flaps closed. Then she fetched Frenchgirl's blanket.

"It will happen faster if you leave the blanket behind." her friend said.

Maggie nodded.

Frenchgirl hauled herself to her feet.

It was hard going, but Maggie helped her along through the deep snow, thinking that maybe she could still do something.

When they reached the tree, a cruel wind came up, whipping the snow around and causing the burial platform to creak overhead.

Maggie lowered her friend to the ground at the base of the tree. They sat around the charred remains of the burial fire, not saying anything, simply listening to the wind and feeling the cold close in all around.

"I'll go now," Frenchgirl said simply. "I'll go to join Cornstalk and my Little Rabbit and my brother Firefly. Sit here with me, Redwing. In this cold it won't take long."

Maggie tried once again, "Let me take you back to the cabin. I can find us some food, I know it. I don't want you to leave."

Frenchgirl looked up at Maggie, "I ask you this as a friend: Let me go. If we had had this conversation ten days ago, I might have listened to you. But it is time.

"Light a fire for me," she said.

Then Frenchgirl settled onto Maggie's lap and closed her eyes.

Maggie sat in the snow with her friend as the sun was climbing in the morning sky. The sun was bright but the air was bitter cold. Maggie began to sing a snatch of a song, a tune from some far-off place, a farewell and a lament and a lullaby all rolled into one.

It was as if she was singing a farewell not just to Frenchgirl, but to everything that had been—to Firefly and Cornstalk, to the young warriors and the clan women, to the old people and the young children, but most of all, farewell to a life that might have been. She wept, despite herself.

Maggie had no way of knowing how long she sat there in the snow, holding her friend and murmuring her farewell song.

Frenchgirl's body had become still and small and lifeless in Maggie's arms. Maggie knew that her friend had gone to the otherworld.

She prepared the body by wrapping it in the blanket and placing it on the scaffold beside Firefly, where the wind and the cold and the weather could turn the bones and flesh back to earth.

Chapter Ten

It had been two days since Maggie had placed Frenchgirl's cold body on the scaffold. And still Jake and Poordevil had not returned.

Instead, the rains came. Cold, freezing rains that pitted the snow and washed it away, turning the ground around the cabin into a slushy pond. The river ice was melting now, causing the river to rise and flood the low-lying fields. It was a miserable time to be cold and hungry.

Maggie hadn't had any real food for four days. After Frenchgirl passed on, Maggie took to eating boiled bark and sipping pine needle tea, a thin, astringent drink made by brewing white pine needles in a kettle of melted snow-water. This was truly starvation food.

Maggie went about her daily tasks in a daze now, sleeping often, never quite waking, sometimes not sure whether she was awake or dreaming. Strange fears came and preyed on her at night. Sometimes she heard sounds outside the cabin. Her nameless fear took shape in the form of wolves. She knew there were wolves up in the hills. But she had never seen any come down into the village. Sometimes at night, lying in her thin blankets by the feeble fire, she thought she could hear wolves scratching at the log walls with their claws. Or walking around on the roof overhead.

Then, one night, she had a strange wolfy dream: She dreamt she was sitting beneath the burial tree, before her tiny fire, when a female timber wolf stole up into the firelight and sat back on its haunches, watching her with interested eyes.

Maggie spoke out into her dream, spoke to the wolf saying, "What do you want from me?"

The wolf didn't answer her, at least not in words. Instead, the she-wolf turned and loped out across the slushy ground for a dozen yards then stopped and turned as if it was waiting for her to follow.

Then Maggie did a strange thing in her dream. For no reason that she could explain, she went down on all fours and began to run as a wolf runs. Within a moment's time, it was as if she had become a wolf herself, loping gracefully up and out of the village, out into the fields and into the snow-covered grasslands beyond.

Maggie thought to herself, "This is what it must be like to run like a wolf."

The ground disappeared under her feet at a rapid rate as she ran, shoulder to shoulder, with the female, loping up through the fields and into a thick stand of aspen trees which stood trembling in the wind. Maggie noticed that in this place the bark had been stripped from the trees.The snow was deep-drifted around the trunks of the saplings. The she-wolf began digging. Maggie dug too, using her forepaws to pull the snow back, using her hind legs to kick it behind her.

Then, her keen wolfy eyes fell on something dark in the whiteness of the drift: the hoof of a whitetail deer, protruding from the snow.

Maggie and the she-wolf dug faster now, uncovering the frozen body of a young doe.

The human part of Maggie knew that this was a deer that had frozen in the early winter and had been covered by the deep drifts. The wolf part of Maggie knew that, frozen or thawed, raw or cooked, this was food. Maggie sunk her teeth into the frozen flesh and satisfied her hunger.

When Maggie shook herself awake the next morning, she knew that her dream hunger had been satisfied. Now she must see to her physical hunger.

She remembered the story Rory had told, about his dream with the dog, and suddenly, a wild idea sprang into her mind: She would follow her dream and find that deer yard, deep-drifted in the aspen stand. Maggie strapped on her belt, with her skinning knife and hatchet, and set out.

Maggie walked to the burial tree and was not altogether surprised to find two sets of wolf tracks leading off into the fields. It was easy following the tracks in the wet snow. There were physical tracks on the ground and there were the landmarks from her dream to guide her as well. In a short time, Maggie floundered up through the wet snow into the stand of aspen.

She dug with her mittened hands in the snow and was amazed, and not amazed, to sweep the whiteness back from the long, thin form of a young doe, frozen with legs outstretched.

Maggie pulled a length of strong cord from her beltpouch and tied it around the doe's neck. She fashioned a loop which slid over her shoulder. She would drag the deer back to the cabin and begin the butchering. Even though the doe was small and it slid well over the wet snow, the dragging was hard work and Maggie had to stop every hundred paces and rest.

In one place, as she was coming down through a stand of

small trees, Maggie caught a glimpse of something sitting upright in the snow. It was the she-wolf. Maggie stood, her breath coming in fast gasps, and locked eyes with the female.

She thought then about her dream, about what it was like to run with the wolf and hunt and smell as a wolf does. For a fleeting moment, she almost wished that she could become a wolf now, leaving this human suffering behind and taking to the hills, to hunt wild and free and join in the wolf songs at night, sleeping warm in leafy hillside dens and playing with the pups in the early morning sunlight. She wished, most of all, that she could become part of it: part of the forest and the snow and the wind that swept the hillsides.

But then that moment passed. She was a human, not a wolf. And she had a boy to find and a deer to butcher. She had human things to do. Maggie drew her hatchet and hacked off the deer's hind legs. She tossed them out into the snow for the wolf.

Then she turned her back and headed for the village.

Thinking back on it later, Maggie wondered if the wolf she had seen was a real wolf or just a ghost-wolf, a dream wolf brought on by some hallucination of starvation.

But whichever it was, the deer she had found was real enough. She drug it back to the cabin and thawed it out by the fire. Remembering the things Frenchgirl had taught her, Maggie respectfully skinned and butcher the deer, slicing the meat thin and setting the internal organs aside for the stew pot.

She ate the first broth of the stew, slowly, savoring the taste. That afternoon, in a sun-melted patch, she found the rising sprigs of the first wild onions and she mixed these with the thin venison, weeping as she remembered Frenchgirl's bag soup, savory with onions.

She used the deer brains to tan the hide. This would be a new set of moccasins.

Sitting by the fire one afternoon, rubbing the hide soft over her knee, she heard a sharp bark.

Poordevil!

Maggie leaped up and pushing aside the cabin door, she could see Poordevil trotting towards her, his ears flopping and his tongue hanging out. Behind the dog, Jake trudged through the wet snow, hauling the toboggan. When they got closer Maggie was astonished to see the butchered remains of an elk tied down on the sled.

Poordevil leaped around in the snow, licking her face and almost knocking her over.

"Get the stew pot on the fire!" Jake hollered. "It's elk steaks, elk grease and elk liver fer dinner!"

He was in good spirits, still flushed from the success of the hunt.

"That's a mighty good bear dog you got there!" Jake said as Maggie helped him haul the toboggan up to the door of the cabin, "He sniffed this fella out in the dense thicket of the cedar swamp. I got 'im with a single shot through the heart and lungs. I figger we got enough meat and fat here to last us through 'til spring! How've you and Frenchgirl done?"

Maggie's smile vanished. Of course, she thought, he doesn't know. It seemed like a long time since Frenchgirl had died.

Maggie told Jake about her companion and how she had

chosen to die.

Jake nodded, "She died well. Died the way she wanted to. Not many of us get to choose the way we're goin' to go."

That night, after a feast of talk and food, Maggie found the strength to walk out to the the tree and light her evening fire. The quiet tragedy of Frenchgirl's death still weighed heavily upon her. But lighting the fire for her journey to the spirit world was a small comfort, just as it had been when Firefly had first died.

Now that Jake and Poordevil were back, and now that her belly was full, she felt herself coming back into the world of human feelings again. The dream with the wolf, the fantastical coincidence of finding the snow-covered deer, and the strange wolfy visions she had shared during her starvation days began to fade. But one thing remained: the joy of running, nose held high, paws touching lightly on the ground, on the night when she had run with the she-wolf. That, she would never forget.

On the following morning, Maggie and her companion made a strange discovery. A terrific ice-storm had swept through the valley in early morning, coating the trees with a thick layer of ice. The smaller branches couldn't bear the weight and hung bruised and twisted. Mid-sized trees had fallen to the ground.

When Maggie took the toboggan down into the thicket by

the river, looking for dry firewood. Poordevil loped along beside her, sniffing at the icy ground. Maggie noticed that a large tree had come down in the storm, narrowly missing the Ragpicker's hut, caving in one side of the structure, shearing off part of the bark cover.

Maggie left her sled and walked over to investigate. When she knelt and looked into the interior of the hut, she was astonished to see that it was packed solid with dry leaves.

Poordevil trotted up beside her and buried his nose and the leaves, snuffling and barking.

"What is it, boy?" Maggie asked.

Strangely, the dog began to dig with his front paws, pulling back the leaves. Maggie drew her knife and cut away a large panel of bark. A cascade of dry leaves spilled out onto the wet ground. A chill wind came up and carried the leaves away, sending them spinning out across the thicket.

Then Maggie saw something curious protruding from the leaf pile: It was a human foot, encased in a weathered, pointy-toed moccasin.

Maggie sprang to her feet, "Jake!" she hollered. "Jake! I need you!"

Up in the village she heard an answering shout and a few moments later the old man came rushing down through the icy

woods, his rifle held ready.

"What is it?" he asked, glancing around the clearing.

Maggie pointed with a trembling finger. "Look..."

Jake knelt and peered into the pile of leaves.

"It's her, ain't it?"

Maggie nodded.

"Well, let's pull back these here leaves and see what we kin see."

Maggie and Jake worked quickly, sweeping back the dried leaves to reveal the small blanket-wrapped figure of the

Ragpicker, laid on her back in the leaves. Her hands were clasped together like the claws on a bird. Her face was covered with a strange mask made from coiled cornhusks, with a nose and mouth hole but no eyes.

"What do you make of it?" Maggie asked.

"I don't rightly know," Jake said, "I s'pose it could be some kinda burial mound. But I never heared of the Seneca buryin' their dead this way."

"But who could have buried her here, and where is Hoot Owl?" Maggie asked, even though she knew Jake didn't have the answers to these questions.

"Think we should just let it be?" Jake asked. "I don't like messin' with someone's burial."

"I don't either," Maggie said, "but maybe there is some clue here, something that will tell me something about Hoot Owl."

Then Maggie knew what she must do: She must crawl up into the leafy pile and lift the mask from the old woman's face. Maggie wiped her hands on her coat and cautiously crept forward. Poordevil sat on his haunches in the snow, watching intently. Maggie knelt in the leaves beside the old woman's head. As she moved into position, her knee struck a large birchbark box. Jake helped her set the box aside so she could reach the old woman's mask. With trembling fingers, Maggie reached down and lifted off the cornhusk mask, peering into the face of the woman she had hunted for so long.

The old woman looked gray and cold, but well-preserved. Her face looked as if it was molded from gray candle wax. Her eyes were closed peacefully and her mouth was set in a thin, almost smiling line.

Then Maggie noticed something. It was so faint that at first she thought it was only her imagination. But then she was sure: a small cloud of warm breath was escaping from the old woman's nostrils!

"Jake, come here. Have a look at this."

The old hunter knelt in the leaves beside her and placed his fingers along the side of the old woman's neck, feeling for her pulse.

"Well, I'll be dogged," Jake exclaimed, "she's alive!"

"But how?"

"I don't know," the old man admitted, "maybe like a bear in hibernation 'er somethin'. The point is, if we're ever gonna find yer boy, we gotta get this woman woked up and talkin'. Let's git her on that sled and git her back to the cabin and thaw her out afore the fire."

Working carefully, Maggie and Jake lifted the old woman up out of the leaves and carried her to the toboggan. As they laid her on the rough wooden surface, Poordevil came over and began licking the old woman's face with his warm, pink tongue.

Then Maggie remembered what had happened that day by the river, when she had fallen through the ice of the Allegheny. She remembered the strange frozen dream and the hot Hemlock bath.

"Jake, I've got an idea! I know how we can thaw her out!"

As they hauled the toboggan back to the cabin, Maggie explained what they could do.

"We'll get some kind of a tub or a—I know!—we can use that dug-out canoe that's propped up against the house down the road, we can drag that in and you get some water boiling on the fire and I'll go out and collect some hemlock boughs—"

They worked furiously for the next hour, dragging the dug-out canoe into the cabin, getting the pots boiling and cutting the frozen clothing off of the old woman with their knives.

She was thin, but did not seem emaciated. Maggie and Jake lowered the old woman down into the dug out and laid her out, full-length. Then they laid in armfuls of fresh hemlock branches and then water, lots of it, adding pot after pot of boiling water. Maggie fetched in buckets of water from the creek. At last, they had the dug-out filled to the brim with steaming, hemlock-tainted water, covering most of the old crone's body.

Remembering her dream, Maggie took a rag and began washing the old woman's feet, rubbing her gray limbs and watching as her bloodblush return, turning her skin from gray to yellow and at last to pink. Poordevil came over and lent his long pink tongue to the job, licking the woman's face and hair.

Jake held the old woman's head above water. At last, her eyes sprang open and her toothless mouth began to work, opening and closing. Jake gently poured a few drops of sassafras tea down her throat. Her eyes began to focus and brighten, as if she were gradually coming back from a place far, far away.

Then a voice began to come up out of her throat. At first, it was nothing more than a hoarse whisper. Jake had to place his ear down by her mouth to hear.

"She's tryin' to tell us somethin'," Jake said, "she's saying somethin' about the boy."

"I didn't know you knew any Seneca, Jake."

"I don't. This here woman ain't speakin' Seneca. She's a Lenape. You 'member, I told you I lived amongst them years ago. I kin pick out a word here and there."

Maggie took the woman's fingertips in her own and began to chafe the skin, encouraging the blood to flow. The woman's eyes were clearing now, as she glanced around in the hemlock mist. Her eyes fell on Maggie. Then her hand came to life, she pointed outside, her ancient mouth working around half-whispered words.

"What is she tryin' to say?" Maggie asked.

"I can't make it out," the old man said," We'll just have to give her time to come around, then we'll figger it out."

It took time for the old woman to move on her own but, at last, she sat up in the bath and gestured for her clothing. Maggie fetched the old woman's ragged blanket -robe and she and Jake helped her stand and slip into it. Steam streamed off the thin crone as she sank onto a deerskin spread out on the floor by the fire. Jake held a cup of tea to her lips.

Her voice was coming out plainer now, plainer and louder. Jake listened intently. At last he nodded.

"We made us a mistake," Jake said, "we left yer boy behind. She says he's wrapped up in a birchbark box she buried in the leaves beside her."

Maggie sprang to her feet. Of course! The box she had struck with her knee.

"I'll go down and fetch it!" Maggie hollered.

Before Jake could answer, she was out the door and running through the wet fields, down into the thicket. Poordevil trotted along beside her. Maggie ran, leaping ice-covered logs and dodging through the debris from the ice storm.

Her mind was working furiously as well, churning out questions: If the old woman had survived, in some kind of hibernation, was it possible that Hoot Owl was still alive? And if he was, could they revive him as they had her?

Maggie ran up to the hut and frantically sifted through the leaves for the box. At last, her hand struck it's angular edge. She hauled it up out of the leaves. It was about the right size, big enough to hold a small child, and heavy. She could see that the lid of the box was punctured with dozens of air holes and that the whole thing was held together by strips of cord wrapped round and round. She clutched the box to her chest and dashed back up into the village.

She and Poordevil pushed their way through the cabin door and stumbled into the firelit room. Jake and the old woman were motioning for her to lay the box by the hearthfire. Jake drew his knife and cut away the cord.

When the Ragpicker lifted off the lid, Maggie gasped aloud.

Chapter Eleven

There, wrapped in a warm rabbitskin, lying on a bed of yellow cornhusks, was the little boy, Hoot Owl. He was gray with cold. Maggie carefully lifted him from the box and held her ear to his chest. Inside his ribcage, like the beating of a slow drum, Maggie could hear rhythm of her little boy's heart.

"He's alive," she breathed, "let's put him in the bath and thaw him out."

"Wait," Jake said, "let's not rush inta this. The old woman and I been talkin' and I think I understand what happened here. It's strange doin's, not doubt about that, but here is what I kin make out: This here's a root-woman and she—"

"A root-woman," Maggie asked, "what's that?"

"Well, she knows about roots and herbs and such and—"

"Like a witch?"

The old man shook his head, "Well, not what we call a witch. As far as I can figger, she don't have no magic powers 'er nuthin'. But she did do somethin' amazin'.

"See, she knows this root what grows in the woods. You chaw on this root and swallow down the root juice and it puts a body inta a deep sleep—kinda like a bear in hibernation."

"You mean she—"

"Yep. She says they lived on wild dogs and scavenged corn all through the early winter and then the food ran out and she figgered this was the only way they'd make it through until spring. So she chewed some of the root and gave the boy some and burrowed down in that leafy hut, hopin' to sleep the winter through. Well, dag-nabit, it looks like they done it."

"She wants to say somethin', Jake."

The old woman said a few words and gestured to the baby.

"She says she's gotta hold the baby before ya put him in the bath."

Cautiously, Maggie handed Hoot Owl over to the old woman, just as she had done so many months before. But this time she would watch and would not lose track of him.

The old woman took Hoot Owl into the folds of her robe, closed her eyes and rocked him for several moments. Gradually, a faint eerie tune came up out of the old woman's lips. Maggie recognized the lullaby she had heard the old woman sing before.

Maggie knew by the expression on the old woman's face that this was more than a simple lullaby. She was concentrating very hard and was singing the song as if she were reaching into another world, into the shadowy, slow-moving world where turtles go when they sleep in the mud, where a bear goes to dream its winter dreams.

At last, the song ended and the old woman opened her eyes, nodding to Jake. Then she handed the baby back to Maggie and gestured toward the tub of steaming water.

Maggie pulled the rabbitskin from around her boy's body and lowered his cold, still body into the hemlock brew. The old woman came and sat beside her, holding the boy's head above water as they washed and rubbed him. Gradually, his skin began to take on life. At last, his leg and arm muscles twitched. His mouth worked convulsively and then in a great gasp, he opened his mouth and let out a high-pitched wail.

Maggie lifted him up out of the bath and onto her shoulder, feeling the welcome bulk of his weight against her. She held him up at arm's length and looked into his eyes, opening now to the firelight.

"Good boy!" she said. She said it over and over until she was satisfied that he was back in the land of the living.

Just then, Poordevil appeared at the doorway. He had run outside again and in all the excitement, no one had noticed that he was foraging around outside. A cloth bag dangled from his mouth.

"What in tarnation is zat?" Jake asked.

Poordevil dropped the sack on the ground.

The old woman became very excited and gestured toward the bag, talking rapidly. Jake fetched her the bag and watched as her trembling bird-like hands pulled open the mouth of the sack and drew out seven cornhusk dolls, one after another, setting them before the fire. Then she fell to talking with them and washing them with a rag and straightening their clothing, going on as if Maggie and Jake were not there.

"She's in another world," Jake murmured.

"Good thing for us she knows about the other world," Maggie said. "I think that's what saved our boy."

Poordevil crept up cautiously and sniffed the small boy. Hoot Owl gurgled happily.

That night, Jake broiled up elk steaks on the fire. Maggie fed Hoot Owl a few spoonfuls of Spook Yeast from her pouch, thinking that the yeasties would be good for him.

The old woman ate heartily and served tiny bits of meat and droplets of grease to her faceless dolls, talking away in her ancient tongue, ignoring Maggie and Jake.

The next morning, when Maggie opened her eyes, she wondered if the whole thing had been imagined. But Hoot Owl was real enough, lying in the crook of her arm, his sweet baby's breath close to her ear.

She sat up and looked around. Poordevil and Jake were there. But the old woman, and her mysterious dolls, were gone. Clutching Hoot Owl to her chest, Maggie stood and pushed her way through the doorway, letting the early morning light stream in.

Out over the treetops, she saw a strange shape, it looked to be an owl, winging its way south, downriver.

Maggie knew. It was time to go back.

She heard Jake blowing on the embers of the fire. Turning, he asked her, "She's gone?"

Maggie nodded. "I wonder if she'll be all right?"

The old man straightened up, brushing his hands off on his pant's leg.

"I wouldn't worry 'bout her, I spec she'll make out just fine. The snow will be meltin' soon and the river will be unfroze, green plants will be comin' up. A person what knows the plants will never be hungry durin' the growin' season."

Maggie stared out across the fields. The owl was gone now.

All things considered, Maggie thought Hoot Owl had come through his ordeal in fine shape: When they got down to Franny's she would put some meat on his bones, get him chubby and frisky for the summer.

Maggie and Jake spent the day drying the meat over the fire. Jake scraped and dried and fashioned the elskin into a pack which he would carry on his back. The snow which made the toboggan slide would be gone any day now, replaced by a slurry of mud and leaves.

It was almost maple sugaring time, Maggie thought

wistfully. If she was still living among the Seneca, this would be the time when the families would take their elm bark buckets and their kettles off into the sugar bushes. They would tap the sap which rose on warm days, late in winter, and boil it down to syrup which would sweeten their lives the whole year through.

When Maggie glanced around the ruined village, she remembered those times. She felt a great longing to turn back the events of the last year, restoring this place to its living state, when the colorful and compassionate people she had known were still living here, still calling this place their home.

But she knew she was powerless to do that. Instead, she was faced with the charred ruins of that life. As the slush melted and revealed more and more of the scorched town, Maggie began to sicken and was anxious to be on their way.

At last, Jake was packed and had stowed the snowshoes and the toboggan in the cabin, leaving them there for anyone who cared to take them.

He drug the heavy pack out into the yard outside the cabin.

"Say yer goodbyes, girl," he said quietly.

Maggie knew what he meant. She knew that she could light one last fire for Frenchgirl and Firefly. With Hoot Owl on her shoulder, Maggie walked down to the tree and sat down beneath it, placing her back against the weathered trunk and glancing up at the scaffold overhead. A few pieces of ragged blanket flapped in the wind.

She drew out her flint and steel and kindled a small fire, no bigger than her hand, and fed it with twigs from the tree. She held Hoot Owl to her and closed her eyes and cried the last tears she had left for her Seneca companions.

Jake was kind. He didn't hurry her. He just waited until she quietly walked up out of the field and into the village. Shouldering his back, Jake stepped ahead, toward the Genesee.

"No sense wadin' the river here," he said, "We may as well walk down on this side fer as long as we kin."

Maggie nodded and they set out.

They camped that night near the bluffs of the gorge. The next day they entered the great gorge and then walked downstream, down the Genesee and out of the Seneca Country.

It was ten days of steady travel, through spotty sunshine and pouring rain, to Rory's cabin on the Allegheny.

Maggie hadn't let herself think much about Rory, or any man, for that matter. She was glad that she was alive and that she had found her boy. That was enough. And that they should get home safe and sound. But she hadn't thought much about a man.

She knew she wanted one, sooner or later. But just as Frenchgirl had said, once she had been a Seneca woman. She wasn't interested in becoming someone's toilslave.

It was while she was thinking these thoughts, while walking south along the Allegheny river trail, that Jake remarked, "We'll be comin' up on Garvin's place any time now. I believe his cabin sets right around that river bend up there. What say we stop and get ourselves cleaned up a bit?"

Maggie furrowed her brow. "Cleaned up?" she asked, "Since when did you ever worry about groomin' yourself?"

"Well," Jake said awkwardly, "what I mean is—Well, what I meant to say was—maybe you would like to just wash yer face and maybe comb them briars out of yer hair—"

"Jake, "Maggie said, a smile playing at her lips, "don't push."

"I ain't pushin' nuthin'. All I said was—"

"I know what you said and yes, thank you, I would like to take a moment."

Jake lowered his pack to the ground by a big rock which jutted out into the river. He made a great show of washing his face and smoothing back his hair. But Maggie knew that this stop was not for him, but for her.

She laid Hoot Owl down against a tree stump. She knelt on a big rock and peered down into a still pool of water. For the first time in weeks, she saw her reflection.

She was shocked. Her face looked thin and weary. Her cheeks were sunken and she was covered with charcoal smears and briar scratches. Her long red hair was filthy, pulled back in a long, lumpy braid that trailed down her back. She had never considered herself a great beauty, but she had always delighted in the feel of her hair, rising and falling in the wind. But now it was clotted with grease and dirt. She hadn't had a proper bath all winter.

She cupped her hands and splashed the cold Allegheny water up into her face, scrubbing away at her skin.

"What am I doin' all this for?" Maggie asked herself, "I'm actin' like a girl at a barn dance. I'm a mother—I'm a widow in fact."

But still, she did her best to scrub away the grease and dirt of

the trial, wanting to look womanly again.

Jake said nothing, he just wiped his hands dry on the front of his buckskin shirt.

"What do you say? Are we ready to shove ahead?" He said at last.

"Ready as I'll ever be."

Maggie swung Hoot Owl up onto her hip and they walked the trail up around the river and into the clearing by Rory's cabin. Somewhere up in the woods, they heard the sound of someone chopping wood.

Chapter Twelve

Rory set down his axe and reached for his horse pistol. He had heard something down by the river. This time of year, he was always wary. He knew the Seneca war parties would be traveling soon and he knew his cabin was right along one of the main warpaths.

Rory knelt down behind a tree and peered down through the forest. His eyes were fine now. The snowblindness had left him without any permanent damage.

He could make out three figures coming up from the river trail. One was an old man, one was a woman with a baby on her hip. A dog trotted ahead of them, sniffing the ground.

Rory smiled and said to himself, "By thunder, they made it!"

He stood up and shoved the pistol into his belt. He retrieved his axe and slung it over his shoulder, ambling down into the clearing.

Maggie knew him from the way he walked. He had a quiet,

sure way of moving, even snowblinded, she could tell that.

"Howdy!" he shouted out.

"We got elk!" Jake hollered back.

"Come along then," Rory motioned towards the cabin.

When Maggie came up to within speaking distance, Rory stopped and nodded.

"I see ya got yer boy, that's good. How'd ya find 'im?"

Maggie grinned. "It's a strange story to tell," she said.

"Well, come on inside, we'll put on the kettle and ya kin tell it all, from beginning 'til the end. It surely is good to see you folks."

Rory did put on the kettle. They made tea and talked and ate and fed the scraps to Poordevil. Rory found a slab of maple sugar to give to Hoot Owl. He sucked on it contentedly.

"I thought you mighta been Indians coming downstream on the war path," Rory said.

"They'll be travelin' soon," Jake said. "Me and Maggie, we're headed down to Kittanning as quick as we kin git there. I don't suppose you'd wanta come with us?"

Maggie gave Jake a sidelong glance.

"Naw," Rory said, "I think I'll stay up here a while, maybe I'll head down later in the spring, if things gets too risky up here."

"Aw, that's too bad," Jake said, "because I was just thinkin' if we had us a canoe we could be down at the tavern in three, four days. Otherwise I guess we'll just have to traipse along, me, with my bad leg and my sore shoulder and Maggie here, a young mother carrying her child. Don't worry about us, sleeping out in the rain and sleet and havin' to feed that baby on short rations—"

Maggie frowned, "Jake stop. It's all right, Rory. It's not all that bad. We'll be home in a week or so and then this whole thing will be behind us."

"You sound like yer a little tired of adventure," Rory remarked.

Maggie laughed, "I'll thank the Lord to never give me any more adventures such as I've had."

Rory smiled. "I know what ya mean. Maybe I am pushin' my luck a little to stay up here any longer. I suppose there wouldn't be no harm in goin' downriver now."

Jake nodded, "That's a smart decision. You won't be sorry fer helpin' us out."

"No," Rory said, "I don't expect I will."

Secretly, Maggie was pleased. But she made a great effort of not showing it.

Maggie glanced around the cabin. She thought about asking about Hank, wondering if Rory's dog had come back. But the answer was obvious and there was no point in bringing it up.

That night, they feasted, playing with the baby in the firelight and fell asleep by the warm glow of the fire.

Rory and Jake worked on the canoe the next morning, overturning it and setting it up on two logs, sealing the cracked seams with melted pine pitch and sewing up any loose pieces with tamarack root lashings.

By noon they were loaded and in the water. Maggie sat in the center with Hoot Owl on her lap. They stowed their few provisions. Jake and Rory paddled in the bow and stern. Poordevil stretched himself out among the gear and they shoved off downstream.

Every paddle stroke brought them closer to Franny's tavern. The water was fast and cold and dangerous. Maggie was impressed by the way Rory and Jake handled the rapids with a quiet courage which didn't require any words, just a stroke and sweep of the paddle in fast water, allowing them to careen past huge boulders and through tight log jams which threatened to smash their craft to splinters.

There were long quiet hours, too, times when the river carried them along easily, when they only had to dip the paddles to keep the craft on course.

At night, they slept under the overturned canoe in riverside camps, rolled up in their bearskins and blankets by a tiny fire.

After four days of paddling, they came within sight of the first cabins and farms. Late in the afternoon on their four day on the river, Maggie glanced ahead and saw the familiar outline of her Aunt Franny's tavern, set on a slight rise above the riverbank.

"We're home," she whispered to Hoot Owl.

Rory and Jake maneuvered the canoe through the fast water and brought it sliding up along the muddy bank, a hundred paces from the cabin door.

"Well, "Jake said, "we did it. Good job on the paddle there, Garvin."

Maggie stepped out into the shallow water and waded up onto the bank, carrying Hoot Owl on her hip. Then she heard a shout.

When Maggie turned, she saw two figures coming towards them, walking fast through the spring mud. One was tall and thin, that would be Uncle Thomas. And one was was built solid, with red hair that shined in the sunlight. That was her Aunt Franny.

Maggie ran to her aunt and fell into her warm embrace, holding Hoot Owl up for her to see.

"So this is the Little Hoot Owl," Franny said in her rough Irish brogue, "we'll put some meat on his bones, I can assure ye of that!"

Uncle Thomas ran down to the shore and helped the men draw the canoe up and tie it safely to a sapling. Poordevil frisked around barking, glad to be back on firm ground.

Maggie and Franny glanced down there.

"Looks like the menfolks are goin' to talk each other's ears off," Maggie's aunt said, "You come inside and I'll get some Callahan Bread inta ye, sure Maggie ye look as thin as kin be...Where'd ye come by thet fine-lookin' dog?"

Maggie laughed, "That's a long story."

"Aye, and ye'll have time to tell it, but first it's bread and drink ye'll need."

Franny did have Callahan bread. She had bread and buttermilk and red turnips. She had venison soup and corncakes and dried apples, all things Maggie had dreamt about in her starvation days.

But now the starvation days were over. She was home, she was really home.

That night, Maggie broke away from the celebration at the tavern and climbed the hillside above Kittanning, looking out across the Allegheny. From where she stood, she could see to the four directions:

To the east, back toward Philadelphia, where she had come from so long ago; to the south, where her home would be; to the north, where she had spent her time in captivity and hardship; and last of all, to the west, to the land of promise.

Maggie knew that out there, beyond the armies and the land-grabbers and the wars, there was free land, free and wild and open, lit by starlight and scoured by wind and snowstorms. She knew that somewhere out there, in the Ohio, there were fresh wild places, where a person could go and be free of whatever was troubling them.

The wind picked up, blowing Maggie's red hair out in the wind. She stood for a long time, gazing out across the rolling Pennsylvania hills, just as she had years ago, when she had first come to the frontier.

Maggie was looking forward to tonight. And the nights and days that would follow. She knew that tonight at the tavern, there would be firelight and candlelight and stories and songs and laughter. There would be mulled cider and groundhog stew and the smell of fresh-baked bread, mingled with the mouth-watering odor of smoked bear hams.

It would be good.

If you enjoyed this book...

You might be interested to know that, although this is the last book in the Bread Sister Series, Robin plans to continue the adventures of Hoot Owl in a new series of upcoming books.

When these will be available, no one knows. He is a highly undomesticated and cantankerous individual and probably won't do anything until he is good and ready.

If you would like to be placed on a mailing list to receive word when additional books are available, drop a line to Groundhog Press.

In the meantime, you may be interested in the other books in the series, *The Bread Sister of Sinking Creek* and *Maggie Among The Seneca*. Groundhog also has a wide selection of other books and recordings by Robin Moore. To receive a mail order form, write to Groundhog Press, Box 181, Springhouse PA 19477.

Afterword

Now that you have read this story, you may be wondering which part is fact and which part is fiction.

I have been criticized by some armchair historians for making Maggie's adventures too far-fetched for modern-day readers to believe. Some critics have written that the hardships and accomplishments of women like Maggie Callahan are "tall tales" and have no basis in fact. I have enjoyed the controversy these books have created.

The truth is this: If our frontier grandmothers had not displayed the type of determination and tenacity depicted in these stories, they never would have stayed alive long enough to have books written about them. Those who feel these stories are "tall tales" have only to read the actual accounts of the women who lived through those rugged times. In the diaries and journals these women left behind, one can find stories as strange, or stranger, than the ones I have told.

My own historical research has been aimed at assuring that the historical and cultural background of the books are correct and as accurate as modern-day research can make them.

I have also included my own first-hand experiences as a wanderer of the woods and as a person who has lived in primitive conditions for many seasons, feeling the bite of the cold and the warmth of the sun on my back, being glad I was alive and alert and able to partake of nature's hard lessons.

Like Maggie, I am grateful for what I've received.

My primary literary sources for this book have been *The Life of Mary Jemison,* by James Seaver; *The Journals of General John Sullivan and His Men,* obtained by special permission from the New York State Historical Society; Over 50 narratives of women captives during the revolution, from the rare book collection of the Rosenbach Institute in Philadelphia; as well as the classic works on the Seneca, Lewis Henry Morgan's *The League of the Iroquois* and Anthony Wallace's work, *The Death and Rebirth of the Seneca.* Most of all, I am thankful for the wisdom and generosity of the Seneca people, who have shared their knowledge and insights with me during my visits to their area.

I was fortunate to be able to visit the places where this story takes place and to walk a portion of Maggie's route along the Allegheny and Genesee Rivers, listening to what the land had to say. It was quite helpful to be able to see the old site of Little

Beard's village, acres and acres of lush corn and bean fields in the beautiful Genesee Valley.

Some readers may be curious about the origins of the "hibernation" motif I used in the last section of the story. As I mention in the story, this was not a traditional Seneca practice. I have been able to find no record of this technique at use among the Seneca.

Instead, the idea came to me by way of a curious and fascinating story which appeared in the April 1940 issue of Yankee Magazine.The article, written by Robert Wilson, recounted a tale he had gleaned from a 100-year old newspaper clipping from a rural Vermont newspaper.

The newspaper article told the strange tale of an isolated community in New England which "froze" some of their members over the winter and resurrected them, Lazarus-like, in the spring.

The newspaper article offers this eye-witness account of their "thawing out":

"Large troughs made of hemlock logs were placed nearby filled with tepid water, into which the bodes were placed separately with the head slightly raised. Boiling water was then poured into the troughs from kettles hung on poles nearby until the water was as hot as I could hold my hand in. Hemlock boughs had been put in the water in such quantities that they had given the water the color of wine.

"After lying in the bath about an hour, color began to return to the bodies, when all hands began rubbing and chafing them. This continued about an hour when a slight twitching of the muscles of the face and limbs, followed by audible gasps, showed that life was not quenched and vitality was returning.

"Spirits were given in small quantities and allowed to trickle down their throats. Soon they could swallow and more was given them when their eyes opened and they began to talk and finally sit up in their bath tubs.

"They were taken out and assisted to the house where after a hearty meal they seemed as well as ever and in nowise injured, but rather refreshed, by their long sleep of four months."

Whether this can be considered a documented historical account, a tall tale or just a fascinating lie, is a debate I will leave to others. As for me, it was enough that it provided the seed for an imaginative story.

Truly, truth can be stranger than fiction.

About The Author

Robin Moore, whose Scotch-Irish ancestors first came to the mountains of Central Pennsylvania nearly 200 years ago, makes his full-time living as a storyteller and storymaker.

Since 1981, he has presented more than three thousand programs and workshops at schools, museums, festivals and on radio and television. In addition to The Bread Sister Trilogy, he has also written *Awakening The Hidden Storyteller,* a how-to book on storytelling for parents and their children.

Before turning to storytelling , Robin worked as a mountain guide, served as a combat soldier in Vietnam, earned a journalism degree at Pennsylvania State University, and worked as a newspaper reporter and magazine editor.

He now lives with his wife, Jacqueline; his children, Jesse and Rachel; and their hound dog, Butterscotch; in a stone farmhouse on a small patch of land in Springhouse, Montgomery County, Pennsylvania.

About The Illustrator

William Sauts Bock has illustrated over 200 books during the past quarter century and has been honored by the American Institute of Graphic Arts. He is a member of the Philadelphia Children's Reading Round Table and an educator of art, books and his Native American (Lenape Indian) culture.

His books include such seemingly diverse subjects as: Richard the Lionhearted; Sam Adams; Tom Sawyer; The Jersey Devil; Pirates and Lincoln; as well as full color sound/ film productions about Lenape Culture, Robinson Crusoe, American Literature, Ancient Greek Culture, and much more.

A graduate of Philadelphia College of Art, he is also a Lutheran minister. He has returned to the ancient Starpath of his Lenape ancestors. He is a lecturer on his art, "Sauts and the Indian Valley Tradition."

He has traveled up and down the Susquehanna River by canoe sketching important Indian sites. An elder woman of his

Wolf Clan kindred gave him and his children the sacred Lenape name, Netamuxwe, "He who walks in the lead." His relations in the Indian Valley (Souderton) call him Sakima.

His art is owned by the U.S. State Department (Washington DC) and the United nations and hangs in the American Ambassadorial residencies worldwide. He was called upon by "Hollywood" for his insights in making the motion picture "The Last of the Mohicans."

Bock lives with his family in Souderton, Pennsylvania.